THE COWBOY UNDER THE MISTLETOE

COWBOY CHRISTMAS, THE MISTLETOE COLLECTION BOOK 2

EDITH MACKENZIE

To my very own cowboy I was lucky enough to find under the Mistletoe

CHAPTER 1

BORA BORA, CHRISTMAS

Kelly tossed her phone on the table beside her as she reclined back against her cabana. The turquoise waters were light panes of shimmering glass beneath azure-blue skies, and the sun-kissed fabric was warm against her lithe, bikini clad body, the balmy ocean breeze whispering across her toasty skin. *I really should put more sunscreen on or I'm gonna burn,* she thought. *Funnily enough, that's not something Quinn has to worry about.* Her best friend, Quinn, could keep her freezing cold Colorado winter. Nothing said Christmas like an over-the-water bure in Bora Bora.

Twisting one of the several delicate chains she wore around her neck and midriff, she languidly waved a hand in the air, signaling her need for the cute waiter. Tray in hand, he made his way over. Kelly enjoyed the way his eyes roved appreciatively over her body. Yep, she still had it.

"Yes, miss?"

"What's your name?"

"Myles." The waiter had the cutest dimples when he smiled.

"Well, Myles, I'd like a Blue Hawaiian decorated with red and green cherries on a stick." *It was Christmas, after all.*

"Yes, miss."

Settling back down, she thought about Quinn again. She wouldn't be surprised if that girl ran off to the freezing wilds of Colorado with her cowboy, and then the next thing everyone would know, she'd probably up and marry him. Markus Jamison had severely underestimated that girl, and Kelly was going to enjoy watching him stew over it at great length. Heck, it was giving her the warm fuzzies just thinking of her pompous boss gnashing his teeth over Quinn's rejection.

The waiter returned with her drink, the colors in the ornate glass a perfect imitation of the ocean waters in front of her ... and a shot of tequila. *Wait, what's this?* Kelly looked up at him, confused. "Myles, honey, I only ordered the cocktail."

"Yes, miss, the man sitting over there asked me to bring it to you." Myles didn't seem too pleased with this turn of events, his dimples having disappeared beside his down-turned mouth.

Kelly lowered her shades, peering over them to get a better look at the fine specimen raising his glass at her in salute from the pool bar. *Merry Christmas to me.*

KELLY SWIRLED the reddish-brown liquor in her glass, breathing deeply of the marvelously expansive aroma. Oak collided with caramel, the spice wrapping smoothly around the fruitiness. It blazed a trail of warmth through her body, the sweetness at odds with the bitterness as she stared moodily out over the calm, dark waters outside her bure. The moon's wan reflection rippled gently under the slight balmy breeze.

She didn't always drink cognac, but when she did, it had to be sinfully expensive. Kelly felt ever so slightly naughty as she sipped her drink, a luxurious languor sliding silkily over her. It had been a delightful afternoon spent with Kyle, her new friend, dancing attendance on her every whim. She wasn't naïve to think he meant anything by it. She'd pegged his type as soon as he'd cast flirtatious eyes her way—always a girl wherever he went, promising her with smoldering looks that she was the only one in his heart, and quick to forget once out of sight. It was a good thing for both of them that she understood the rules of the game and was a no-strings-attached kind of girl herself. If he was lucky, she might even let him whisper pretty things into her ear again tomorrow.

Geeze, what now? Kelly rolled her eyes as she saw Lachlan's name flashing on her phone. What didn't her boss understand about her being on holidays? "Hello, Lachlan, I'm having a fabulous break from the casino, thank you."

Smug satisfaction filled her at the startled pause on the other end of the line. "Kelly, I'm sorry that you have to play intermediary, but Quinn isn't answering her phone."

"I can't say I blame her. She's on holidays, too. Give the girl a break." *Why was it so hard to get through their heads that Quinn didn't want to be interrupted?*

"Have you spoken to her?"

Oh, I'm going to enjoy this. "Yes, I have, and here's where it's at, Lachlan. She doesn't care. She's not coming back for some overbearing whale puffed up on his own importance."

More silence. "You know this means she won't have a job to come back to, right?"

Oh, please. Here comes the big ultimatum. "I doubt very much that she cares, Lachlan. She's in love. Markus can power trip all he wants, but she isn't going to leave Jackson—especially at Christmas—for him. Power to her." It was gratifying to hear Lachlan spluttering on the other end of the phone. Cutting overbearing men down to size actually went quite well with her cognac. "But let me be very clear, if she does still want her job, she had better have one."

"It's out of my hands. Markus owns The Chimera now, and I doubt very much he'll agree to that. You know what he's like."

Ah, now he's playing the bluff. Two can play at that. "Then he can get himself a new PR and Marketing Manager."

"Is that an ultimatum?" There was an edge to Lachlan's voice.

My, but this wonderful cognac goes so very well with the crow these bullying men are about to eat. "You can call it whatever you want. But please be sure to be very clear when you explain exactly what skills I have and what I've done for The Chimera when you talk to Markus, because I won't be leaving Vegas when I'm no longer employed by The Chimera. I'll be going straight to the competition, and you know just how good I am at what I do."

"I'll tell him."

Kelly swirled her cognac. *It really did smell amazing,* she could imagine her boss on the other end, beet red with frustration. "Oh, and Lachlan?"

"Yes?" he ground out.

"I'm sorry you have to play intermediary, but you know how it is." The line went dead, and Kelly sipped her drink smugly. It really was an excellent drop.

~

QUINN HAD SOUNDED SO childlike in her excitement of having a white Christmas that it had been impossible to not get caught up in it the previous evening. Idly, Kelly applied more lotion to her alabaster skin, inspecting it for any imperfections. *I wonder if it's still as cold and wet as I remember.* It had been years since she'd spent her holidays anywhere other than alone in Bora Bora, not that her family ever invited her home anyway. *I wonder what Dad's doing, or if he ever misses me.* The calm cerulean waters surrounding the bure's deck soothed away the anguish that rippled to the surface of her mind.

The harsh ring of her phone shattered the tranquility. *For Pete's sake, I'm trying to be all Zen here.* Huffing, she picked it up, fumbled, and almost dropped it, having forgotten her hands were still slippery from the lotion. Seeing Markus's number on the screen, she paused, torn. *If I throw it into the ocean now, I can tell everyone it was just a dreadful accident and I had to suffer through the rest of my holidays uncontactable.* Kelly pursed her lips, eyes narrowed against the glare of the sun. *Better not.*

"Hello, Markus. I assume you're calling me to make sure I'm enjoying myself on this gorgeous, sunny Christmas Eve?"

"I don't really care what you get up to on your time off, but I do care about you threatening me." Markus's voice was oily smooth, urbanely masking the venom. Just like the slippery snake he was.

"What, little ol' me?" Her hand rested against her heart. "That's hardly a civilized thing to do at Christmastime. Are you sure you're not confused?"

"I don't have time for games, Kelly. Did you threaten to help out my competition?"

Kelly's lips quirked. *This is going to be fun.* "I was just telling him how it would be if Quinn suddenly finds herself without a job if she still wants one." Silence. Nothing but the gentle lapping of the waves against the piers beneath her. "Hello? Markus, my dear, are you still there?"

"Fine, she can have her job if she wants it. But she better keep that hick cowboy of hers away."

This time when the phone went silent, it was final. Kelly laid back, enjoying the warmth of the sun lounge against her bare back, the briny air filling her lungs. *Don't mess with the big girls, Markus. Not unless you want to lose.*

"MERRY CHRISTMAS." Kelly could imagine Quinn in that awful sweater she'd bought just before she left, sitting with a cup of hot cocoa in front of a roaring fireplace. Judging from all the noise in the background, her boyfriend, Jackson, had quite the large family.

"Merry Christmas. Are you having a good day?"

Kelly stretched her long legs out, surveying her watery domain. "I'm having a good Christmas. Later I'll be having an exquisite seafood platter delivered, and tonight I have a festive nightcap planned with a very virile man. Maybe he'll show me what Santa left in his stocking."

"Kelly!" Quinn laughed. "Oh my gosh, I have so much to tell you."

Quinn was always such a drama llama. "How much could have happened? We only spoke yesterday."

"Well, you're now an aunt. Duchess had her kittens—two boys and three girls. She went out into the snow last night on Christmas Eve, and Jackson and I had to find her. But she was safe with the dog."

"Trust Duchess to be such a dramatic. Awesome, more

furballs to have around the suite." Kelly found herself strangely looking forward to meeting the kittens.

"I've actually arranged for them to live here. I mean, I have to move out of our suite now that I'm not working at The Chimera anymore." There was a catch in Quinn's voice, an odd mix of longing, sadness and, if Kelly wasn't mistaken—and she rarely was—excitement. *What on earth? What hasn't she told me?*

"I talked to Markus, and you have a job if you want it." Kelly held her breath. *Come on, Quinn. You know you want it.* She picked at a pulled thread on her towel.

"Um." Kelly's stomach knotted at her friend's hesitation. "Well, Jackson and I just kinda assumed that I wouldn't be welcome back. And you know, I didn't really like being a hostess to the high rollers. I was thinking I might stay here."

Kelly felt too warm, her vision blurring. "What are you going to do for a job?"

"I hadn't actually thought that far ahead." *Typical Quinn.*

"What if you didn't have to be a hostess anymore? Just be my assistant?"

"I did like that part of the job, and obviously I did it back in Australia with you and I was quite good at it." Quinn's voice brightened, and then fell again. "But Jackson lives here in Colorado."

"Maybe you could do the job part-time? Like, work a few days in Vegas with me, and then do the rest remotely from the ranch?" Kelly crossed her fingers. Seriously, she was offering her one heck of a deal.

"I'd like that, but I have to talk to Jackson first." The noise in the background got louder. "I have to go. We're about to start charades. Merry Christmas, Kelly."

"Merry Christmas." Kelly wasn't even sure Quinn heard it before the line went dead. Tossing the phone onto her sun lounge, she stood abruptly and, with a few quick steps, dove sleekly into the crystal sea. The warm saltwater washed away the hurt Quinn's lack of enthusiasm had caused. Quinn had Jackson now, and Kelly was happy for her. But here, in her self-imposed isolation, it felt like she was being abandoned all over again.

CHAPTER 2

The rigging apparatus slid across the ceiling of the stage as though the rails were made of silk. Suspended from it was a stand-in for the star performer, testing the suitability of the setup. All around was a hive of activity, and with that many people working, the margin for error was greatly increased. Kelly nodded, satisfied that everything was going to her meticulous plan. It was the only thing that saved her sanity when they were doing a swap out of acts at The Chimera.

"I think there should only be minimal changes at this stage," she said, handing her clipboard to Quinn.

"If you have a minute, can we quickly go over the rider for the show? I have a few questions." Quinn scrunched up her face. "And by a few, I mean a few what-on-earth type questions."

"I have a meeting with the head honchos, but if you want to walk with me, I'll try to answer as many as I can." Kelly was grateful to have something to take her mind off the shark tank she was headed to. She always felt like the men were waiting to draw blood—her blood.

"They have asked that I only get fluro jellybeans. I've looked everywhere, and I can't find any. At this point, I'm not even sure they exist." Quinn rolled her eyes, blowing out her cheeks in exasperation.

"Get some white ones and set up a black UV light above it. It might not be exactly fluro, but they will glow. Most of the time, they put these outlandish things on their rider just as a challenge. I had one act tell me that they did it so that, if everything was met, they knew there was an extreme amount of attention to detail paid. I've always remembered that."

"They also asked that only wait staff between the heights of five foot two and five foot four attend them in their dressing room." Quinn tapped the side of her mouth with her pen. "Um, can we even do that without discriminating?"

"I think if we pull them from the staff we already have at the casino, we should be fine. Also, can you please order all the staff who will be working the dressing room new name badges, I want them to have their name and height." *You want attention to detail, I'll give you attention to detail.* Kelly paused at the conference room door. On the other side, she would be going into battle, but it was no different to any other time she'd entered the testosterone-fueled lion's den. "Is that everything?"

Quinn nodded, looking down at her notes. "Yep. I'll get this sorted before I leave. Unless you need me to stay a few days? I can give Jackson a call and let him know."

"No way. I know you'll get it done, and you work from home when you're in Colorado anyway. Go home to your cowboy. I'm sure he's been missing you."

Quinn smiled gratefully. "Thanks."

Kelly took a deep breath, smoothing down her skirt. "Well, time to go poke the bear." Head high and shoulders thrown back, she opened the door and strutted across the polished Italian marble tiled floor, her heels sounding out a machine gun staccato. Everything in the conference room was hard, cold and shiny. *Kinda like the men. Well, Nate's not too bad.*

Markus, the owner of The Chimera had assumed the position of power at the head of the long, black glass table. Lachlan, head of operations, was at his immediate right, and Eddie, the pit boss, was to his left. Everyone was already there except for Nate, the steely eyed head of security. Briefly, Kelly wondered if he was off neutralizing someone. Even without him, the room positively reeked of male power and intimidation. The message was loud and clear. It was a boy's club—one that they suffered her presence in, but one she would never be a card-carrying member of. Kelly smiled smoothly, keeping her features bland. "Good morning, gentlemen."

"Nice of you to join us." Markus smiled, presenting an image of courtesy, but reeking of patronization.

"I thought so." She settled herself in the chair beside Lachlan—all the better to smile at and bait Eddie across the table.

"I had to take care of something," Nate said by way of explanation as he strode into the room and took his place.

"We can begin then," Markus declared, his lips stretched into a thin smile. "Lachlan, if you will start."

Kelly took notes. In her business, she made sure she had information on everything. *And everyone. You never know when you might need it to negotiate for something else.* After what was a fairly longwinded presentation, Lachlan wrapped up his report and turned expectantly to his boss. Markus stood, striding over to the floor-to-ceiling glass windows. *Fancies himself as the lord looking down on the peasants.*

"Thank you, Lachlan. Kelly, would you like to report next?" His voice cut through the expectant silence.

"We're finalizing the equipment and infrastructure for the new act that will be bumping into the Spectrum Theater in a few weeks' time. The promotional campaigns we've been running have exceeded expectations, and we're currently booked out for the first three months of performances." Kelly allowed herself to show a small level of smugness. "I imagine that by the time they open, we should've blown that out to six months."

"We should be at six months now." Markus didn't even bother turning his head to address her, his contemptuous tone sparking her annoyance. She quickly stifled it before it could bloom on her face.

"All shows prior to my arrival were only booked out one month in advance. Since I've started, we've had a steady increase to get to this point," Kelly replied with deceptive calm, irritation beginning to bubble over inside of her, despite her best efforts.

Markus shrugged dismissively, her hard work of little importance to him. "I don't care what happened before I owned The Chimera. All I care about is now." There was a critical tone to his voice. Finally, he turned to spear her with a condescending glare, his eyes flat, hard and passionless. "This level of mediocrity is unacceptable to me. From now on, if all shows aren't sold out nine months in advance you are to consider it a failure. Do you think you can manage that, or would you like a man to help you?" Kelly lifted her chin to meet his icy stare straight on. Dismissing her, Markus's focus turned to Eddie. "What have you got to report to me?"

How dare he speak to me like that. Aware that she was in

danger of snapping her pen, she forced herself to calmly place it down, perfectly parallel to her notepad. She liked things to be ordered and symmetrical, kind of like the crime scene she was fantasizing about in her head with Markus as the star. Kelly plastered a bland smile on her face, nodding as Eddie launched into his spiel. *One day, I'm going to wipe that smirk off his face.*

THE WASH of colors spilled from the ceiling, cascading along the wall to where it pooled in crystalline splendor. The scarlet reds, ambers, oranges and brilliant yellows flickered and swirled as if the artist had captured fire and somehow managed to sheath it in glass. Knowing Evelyn, the artist, Kelly wouldn't put that sort of wizardry past her.

Kelly reverently touched the cool smooth surface, tracing its patterns, breathing in the calmness the sculpture inspired in her. *Some people have Zen gardens, I have Zen glass.* Since the piece's installation, she had witnessed many people's reaction to it. Some stood transfixed by the hypnotic eddy and flow of the liquid flame coiled inside. Others marveled at the energy they claimed to feel ripple from it. No one felt the sublime calmness emanate from it the way she did. Perhaps that was why Evelyn was such a sought-after artist—her work spoke to people on different levels.

Kelly breathed, allowing the coolness beneath her hand to ease the seething frustration that lashed her soul. Business had always been a man's world and she was proud that she could hold her own in it. But darn it all if it wasn't exhausting to constantly have to prove yourself each and every time with everyone waiting, eyes burning fiercely with anticipation that she would mess up and topple from her lofty perch.

"Kelly?" Julie's voice was softly hesitant.

Drawing in one last breath, Kelly smiled wanly at the until recently concierge. "Yes, Julie?"

"I have some high rollers coming in who have requested an all access pass to see the dress rehearsal for the new act. What should I tell them?"

"If you let me know when they want it, I'll escort them there myself."

"Thanks, Kelly. Are you nearly finished for the day?" Julie peered at Kelly, her eyes narrowing speculatively. *I must look wrecked if she's looking at me like that.* "If it will make you feel better, Markus has already left for Monaco."

Kelly rolled her head on her shoulders, welcome relief flooding her. "You have no idea how much better that makes me feel." She eyed Julie knowingly. "Are you regretting giving up your concierge gig to play hostess to the high rollers? I know Quinn couldn't hand it over fast enough."

"I love it. Plus, Quinn is such a pretty little thing, I think that made it a lot harder for her. I'm a whole lot more woman for them to push around." Julie put her hands on her ample hips.

"I'd pay good money to see someone try. I think I'm going to head up to my suite now. Everything should be under control, but you know where to find me if it isn't."

A short elevator ride and she was in the sanctuary of home. The tantalizing ripe fragrance of red wine promised to help her unwind as she brought it to her nose. All the furniture was the same from the day she and Quinn had moved in a year earlier, but since her best friend had fallen in love and spent most of her time in Colorado, it felt colder, more impersonal. Sure, Quinn still spent a portion of each week there, but now the only thing she had was a suitcase of work clothes. Everything else—her little knickknacks and that annoying furball of a cat, Duchess—was now ensconced in the house Jackson had built them.

If she had a heart, she'd almost think she was lonely. *Thank goodness I decided years ago not to have one.* Kelly raised the glass, the lights from the manic street scene below her flickering on the reflection of the window. She didn't even bother to entertain the notion that she missed her best friend. After all, her number one rule was to never get attached. *And I never have.*

CHAPTER 3

The wheels on the overnight suitcase whirred as they spun rapidly across the smooth polished tiles, Kelly's pace brisk. "Kelly!" called Marie, the head pastry chef of The Chimera. "I made this for Quinn."

Kelly stood motionless in the middle of the foyer, waiting for Marie to catch up. *I should have expected this.* Quinn was the type of person who made friends wherever she went, and once word had gotten out that Kelly was headed out to Colorado to attend the surprise birthday party Jackson was throwing her, well, everyone wanted to add something to her luggage. Julie had sent a small blue box tied with a white ribbon. Judging by its size and weight, it was some sort of jewelry. Nate had sent a pen that could be linked to her phone to find it if she ever lost it. She suspected it might also be able to be used as a weapon or turn into an umbrella. And now this. This one looked like it was going to be the icing on the cake, literally. *I wonder if I would command such devotion.*

"I know everything is probably already planned and catered, but I couldn't imagine Quinn having her birthday party and one of my cakes not being there. I hope she likes it."

Kelly juggled the large box in one hand. *This is a seriously heavy cake.* "I'm sure she'll love it. I'll even make sure I take lots of pics so you can see her reaction yourself."

An open, friendly smile overtook Marie's features. "I'd love that. Please tell Quinn happy birthday for me and I'll buy her a birthday drink when she comes back next week."

"I'll be sure to tell her. And you do know she only likes the expensive cocktails?"

Marie giggled. "I don't think I can afford the drinks Markus tried to bribe her with."

Carefully balancing the box on her luggage, she checked the time on her watch. *Darn but I love how the diamonds sparkle.* "Marie, I'm going to have to love you and leave you if I have any hope of getting to the airport in time to catch my flight."

"Of course. Have a safe flight."

Marie waved and headed back to the kitchen, no doubt to whip up more confectionary masterpieces. Securing the cake box under one arm and snagging the handle of her luggage with the other, Kelly strode briskly across the foyer to her waiting town car.

Her name was handwritten in large black lettering on what looked to be a piece of cardboard torn from a packing box. Kelly could feel her eyebrows disappearing into her hairline. *What sort of driver has Jackson sent?* Startling sapphire blue eyes met her disbelieving ones, unruly black curls sitting atop a face that had a sharply chiseled jawline, only slightly outdone by the striking cheekbones. A broad smile showed a mouthful of white, straight teeth. She found it impossible not to return his easy smile.

"I'm Kelly."

He thrust out a hand, dirt beneath his nails. "I'm Wyatt. Jackson asked me to pick you up."

Kelly extracted her hand from his grip and gingerly wiped them on the leg of her pants. "Thank you." She passed the handle of her bag to him, keeping the cake box firmly in hand. "This is all the luggage I have." His dark brows drew together, and he gaped blankly at her. *Maybe he's a bit simple? That would certainly explain his state of dress.* "This is all I have. You can take me to the car now." She stressed each word, speaking slowly so he might better understand her.

Those blue eyes hardened to ice, a muscle jerking in his jaw. "Right this way, princess." He snatched the handle out of her grasp, spun on his heels and strode toward the exit. Kelly almost had to run to keep up with him, holding her cake box tightly. *He better not make me ruin this cake, not after getting it all the way here safely.* Outside they went, confusion making her stride slow as they didn't head to the valet parking as she'd anticipated, instead going to the public parking.

"Excuse me, but are we going the right way?"

"Lady, I know where I parked my own darn truck," he growled.

Truck? Kelly skidded to a halt when her driver picked up her leather embossed luggage and hauled it into the back of a dented, battle-scarred pickup that had clearly seen better days. *More like several decades ago, and not in an awesome vintage way either.* "Careful, that's worth more than your truck."

Hands snagged slim hips as he rounded on her. "Who spends more than a car on luggage?"

"Who drives such a beat-up piece of junk?" Seriously, she

was going to give this driver a one-star review as soon as she could safely put the cake down.

"Just get in the truck, princess," the driver countered in a tense, clipped voice that forbade any further questions.

The door creaked in protest so much that Kelly feared it was in danger of falling off its hinges. Her driver moved a large box that looked like it was filled with bandages and an assortment of bottles and spray packs off her seat and gestured impatiently for her to sit. The springs underneath her twanged as her weight settled. Grimly, she gripped the cake box. *There is no way I'm going to let Jackson pay for this crumby driver service. I can't believe he's still in business.* Staring straight ahead, she pressed her lips disapprovingly into a straight line as gears ground and they lurched into motion. This is why she never strayed too far from the city lights.

The driver felt no need to make small talk, which was perfectly fine with her. Some people always felt the need to fill empty space with clutter or, in this case, chatter. More people needed to learn to value silence as far as she was concerned. At last, they turned off the road and proceeded to make their way down what looked to be a freshly graded dirt drive. In the distance, she could make out several houses and a couple of barns that also appeared to have had recent maintenance and fairly shone with cheery redness. To her surprise, instead of coming to a halt in front of one of the houses, her driver instead followed the drive past them and down a laneway toward a house that stood apart.

There was a neat little white picket fence, large windows overlooking the front yard and a porch that ran along the length of the front of it. Finally, the truck ground to a halt and, after a moment of wrestling with her door, she gained her freedom, exploding out of the truck in a most unladylike manner.

Jackson walked around from the side of the house,

wiping his hands carefully on a rag. "Hello, Kelly." He kissed her on the cheek. "Thank you for coming for Quinn's party."

A smile found its way past the trauma of her experience at the hands of the rude driver. She'd always liked Jackson. "There's no way in the world I'd miss this."

Jackson looked past her and held his hand out to the driver. Kelly drew in a deep breath, ready to inform him of exactly how appalling the service was that she'd just had to endure. "Thanks, Wyatt. I really appreciate you doing this. Wouldn't you know it, I've just managed to fix the problem with my truck."

The front door of the house sprung open and Quinn, her sandy-blonde hair flying behind her, launched herself at her friend. "Kelly! Oh my gosh, what are you doing here?"

Kelly's breath squeezed from her lungs under the vigorous onslaught from her best friend. "Ask your boyfriend," she managed to wheeze out. *Gosh I hope this cake survives till the party., I'm beginning to think the universe is against it.*

Quinn folded her arms across her chest. "Well?"

Jackson smiled, the delight that he'd managed to fool his girlfriend for so long clearly evident on his handsome features. "I thought you might want to have your best friend here for your birthday party is all."

"Oh, Jackson, you're the best. I love you so much." Quinn threw herself into Jackson's arms and kissed him soundly. Clearly satisfied that she'd thanked him sufficiently, she turned to the driver. "I assume you were in on the surprise too, Wyatt?"

"Yes, ma'am." He touched the brim of his hat with his fingers.

"I'm so glad that you've both gotten the chance to meet each other. I just knew my best friend and Jackson's best friend would hit it off."

Kelly looked at the driver-slash-Wyatt with dawning horror. "So, you didn't arrange a driver to come and collect me?" She pleaded with Jackson to tell her otherwise.

"Who organizes a driver? You just pick people up from the airport yourself, or in this case, if your truck breaks down, you ask a friend," Jackson said, looking at her like he was explaining how to make a sandwich to an adult.

"You're Jackson's best friend?" This was beginning to feel like a bad dream. Kelly was becoming uncomfortably aware that she might have made an ill-advised assumption. One that didn't necessarily paint her in the best light.

"Guilty as charged, princess," Wyatt answered with staid calmness, a mocking look on his smug face.

Kelly could feel heat rising up her neck and to her face. "Why didn't you say anything?"

"I said I was Wyatt." He placed his hands belligerently on his hips.

"How was I to know that meant you were his friend?" How dare he stand there looking at her like that.

"Who just assumes I'm a driver?"

"Most of the people I know would."

He leaned in close, his eyes glittering with derision. "Well, princess, you and I live in very different worlds."

"Thank goodness for that." Dismissively, she turned her back on him and linked her arm with Quinn's. "Now, birthday girl, let's go inside so you can see this cake Marie made you. I've carted it all over the place and I'm dying to see it myself." Giving her hips an extra sashay, she brushed the annoying thought that she'd just made a fool out of herself from her mind. *He's nothing but a country hick anyway.* With a final flounce, she followed her friend into the house.

~

Fairy lights set in old mason jars hung from the rafters and every spare corner and space of the old red barn. Wyatt couldn't remember it ever looking fancy—or clean, for that matter. *Jackson sure must love this girl to go to all this trouble.* Fact was, Wyatt could see it with his own eyes just how much the two of them cared for each other. Quinn was one heck of a girl. Beautiful, smart, and since he'd known her, had handled everything the Gregory clan had thrown her way with a smile. What he couldn't figure out is how she had such a stuck-up pretentious friend as the princess he'd picked up from the airport.

Mrs Gregory and the rest of the ladies had outdone themselves, and the trestle tables fairly groaned under the food they'd set out. In pride of place was a cake that had been made to look like a handbag. Wyatt wasn't sure why anyone would want a handbag cake, but if they did, this one looked like the real deal. All the ladies had oohed and aahed when it had been taken out of its box. A box that looked remarkably similar to the one his unappreciative passenger had cradled so protectively the day before.

Unbidden, his eyes looked across the packed earth floor to where she stood, her platinum hair sleek down her back. Wyatt couldn't help but notice when he'd picked her up from the airport how big her pale gray-blue eyes had been. *Even when she was looking down that pert little nose of hers.* What, with her alabaster skin and plum pale lips, there had been an earthly and otherworldly beauty to her. *Pity she was such a stone-cold b—*

"Wyatt, I need you to get everyone's attention for me." Jackson clapped him on the shoulder, jerking him away from his appraisal. "That is, if you're finished looking at all the pretty ladies. Or should I say, one in particular."

The beer caught in Wyatt's throat. "Say what?" He coughed and spluttered.

"I've been watching you. I mean, she sure is a pretty little thing, but not your usual type at all. I thought you liked them brunette and with some meat on their bones."

"Trust me, you couldn't even pay me to have her be my type." Wyatt moved his shoulders in a shrug of anger. "Can you believe she thought I was the driver? What sort of princess is she?"

Wyatt's vehement denial seemed to amuse his friend, adding to his irritation, and he narrowed his eyes in annoyance. "You have to remember that Kelly—and Quinn, for that matter—come from a very different world to us. In that world, it would be completely natural that a limo or town car would be sent for her. And I can imagine what she thought when she saw your beaten-up old truck." Jackson chuckled. "She would've been horrified." The chuckles got louder, and he threw his head back and roared in laughter.

Wyatt was irked by his friend's enjoyment of the situation. There was nothing wrong with his truck! Every time he turned the key, it started, and he could always count on it to get him from A to B. *If you need a car to do more than that, you've got more money than sense.* "Yeah, well, Quinn might come from that world, but she's a sweetheart. This other one is nothing but a judgmental snob. How the heck did they even become best friends?"

"You'd have to ask Quinn for the full story, but Kelly has been a good friend to her and helped her get away from a real bad situation with her ex. Maybe you just need to give her a chance. I know you guys didn't get off to the best start, but surely you can lay on the charm and bring her around."

Once again, he found himself staring at her. Perhaps feeling his gaze on her, she turned, and their eyes connected across the room. *Dang, but a man could get lost in those eyes.* Brows raised haughtily, she turned her back on him, returning to her conversation. "Yeah, I'm not sure she's worth the effort."

"Well, play nice, because I'm about to do something that's kinda a big deal. Now, can you please help me get everyone's attention?"

"Fine." Wyatt wet his lips, raising his fingers to them. Drawing in a deep breath, he let out an ear-piercing whistle. The room went silent, heads whipping around to pinpoint the source.

"Thanks," Jackson muttered dryly.

"Don't mention it." Stepping forward, he held his hand high in the air. "Friends, family"—his gaze strayed to Kelly —"others." He noted in satisfaction that her eyes narrowed in annoyance. *I guess no one said she's dumb.* "My best bud here"—Wyatt clamped a hand on Jackson's shoulder—"has asked me to get everyone's attention. Now that I see I've managed to do just that, I'm going to let him take the floor." With a little flourish, he stepped to one side.

Jackson swallowed, his Adam's apple bobbing. *Dude hasn't looked this nervous since he asked Lisa Mathers to Senior Prom.* He walked forward until he could gather up Quinn's hand in his own. "Quinn, I'm so thankful that you're here with me celebrating your birthday. I know you wanted your parents to be able to be here, but I hope that you're beginning to feel like my family is your family, too." Quinn smiled, looking over at the group of Gregory's and nodded. "And I hope that you and I can have a family of our own one day." Quinn's hand flew to her mouth, huge shocked eyes shimmering with tears when Jackson dropped down on bended knee in front of her. "Quinn Williamson, I know we haven't known each other a long time, but my heart feels like it has known you forever. Will you marry me?"

"Yes!" Quinn held her trembling hand out. Wyatt was amused to see Jackson's work-roughened hand shaking just as much. *If those two don't calm down, ain't no way he's ever going to get that ring on.* At last it slid home, and she threw herself into Jackson's arms, not waiting for him to rise to his feet. Wyatt had noticed that Quinn had a tendency to throw herself at people when she was happy.

"I'd like to raise a glass," a crisp, cool voice said. *I should have known she would find a way to be center of attention.* Kelly stood with her champagne glass out in front of her. "To my best friend in the world and the man who makes her the happiest I've ever seen her. Congratulations."

Everyone toasted, and as he sipped his drink, Jackson eyed her over his glass. Kelly quirked her brows at him smugly. *Two can play at this.*

"I'd like to say something, too." Silence fell. "My best bud has finally found a woman who will put up with him. Quinn, I hope you know what you're getting yourself in for."

Quinn gave a little giggle, blushing in Jackson's arms. "I think so."

"Well then, don't say you haven't been warned, and congratulations." He raised his glass high. Kelly rolled her eyes in disgust, probably at his uncouthness. Wyatt kissed the air. *Bring it, princess.*

CHAPTER 4

Several things offended Kelly about the middle-aged man sitting opposite her. The fact he'd decided to team the garishly patterned silk shirt with the white suit was top of the list, then there was the matter that he'd decided to forego socks with his loafers. It just wasn't hygienic as far as she was concerned. *No one likes smelly feet.* Now he fussed with the cuff of his suit, and with his mouth pursed, he gave it his undivided attention. Which would have been fine if he wasn't there to have a meeting with her.

"Will you be finished anytime soon?" she asked tartly, her stare drilling into him.

With a last adjustment, he tugged it into a place that finally met his obviously high standards of personal grooming. "I think you will find that Mason Cooper has similarly high standards."

"I think you'll find that I've dealt with more than my fair share of aging Hollywood former leading men who now chase the fading limelight all the way to Vegas. I know exactly what sort of standards he has." Kelly leaned forward, steepling her fingers together on the cold glass surface of the impersonal conference room. "I think you will find that what we are offering is very fair given the current relevancy of Mr Cooper. However, if he isn't interested, I have several other performers who have already offered to take the available dates. I only approached you out of respect for Mr Cooper's previous work in his prime." Kelly made a show of gathering up her things. *Three, two, one.*

"Let's not be too hasty. Mason holds The Chimera in highest esteem." It was gratifying to see the self-absorbed smugness wiped right off the fussy little man's face. *Is he sweating?*

"I suggest that you take the terms we're offering to Mr Cooper and, if he's agreeable, that he doesn't dally too long in getting his lawyers to look them over and sign." Kelly pasted on a smile of nonchalance, rising fluidly from her chair. "Now, you'll have to excuse me. I have some other matters that require my attention." With a springy bounce in her step, she exited the room.

From behind her, she heard a hurried, "We'll be in contact."

Men always have to have the last word. Not bothering to slow her pace and her lips curved, displaying her satisfaction, she headed to the elevator.

THE FORK SCRAPED along the plate, cleaning it of the last few morsels of pasta. Kelly rarely allowed herself the luxury of carbs, but when she weakened, she made bloody sure she ate every last drop of it. Sighing in contentment, she walked over to the kitchen. *Why is it that everything that's bad for you tastes so good?*

The thump of the front door made her hastily drop the dish in the sink, rubbing her hands anxiously on the washcloth to remove any last traces. The enjoyment she'd been basking in from the meal disappeared in a swirl of stomach-churning memories. She swore she could hear her mother's voice chastising her. *Chubby girls don't have the luxury to eat for taste.*

"Is anyone home?" Quinn called, trundling her luggage behind her.

"Hey, I thought you weren't coming till tomorrow morning." Kelly went to give her a hug, leaving the cold memories behind her in the kitchen.

"I was, but Jackson has to help Wyatt pick up some horses." Quinn's eyes sparkled and her lips were pressed tightly together, though she wasn't entirely successful in stopping the corners of her mouth from twitching. *That girl looks like she's about to explode.* "Plus, it will give us a chance to hang out. We don't get to do that anymore." *Yep, she definitely had something to say.*

"Sure thing. Get yourself sorted and then come and have some wine with me." Kelly picked up the empty bottle. "Actually, I might need to order another one."

"I need to ask you something first. I can't hold it in any longer." Quinn shook her balled fist.

Kelly's brow rose. "Should I sit down for this?"

"Yes. No. Yes."

Kelly grinned at her friend's barely suppressed excitement. "Which one?"

"Yes, sit down. But hurry." Her friend bounced on the balls of her feet.

Kelly made a show of slowly taking her time to comply, enjoying the look of impatience that flitted across Quinn's face. "All right, I'm ready. What would you like to ask me?"

The cushions of the sofa sunk under Quinn's weight as she sat beside her. "Well, first, Jackson and I have settled on a date for the wedding. It's going to be Christmas Eve. It was such a special day and holds a lot of meaning for both of us."

"Wow, congratulations." Kelly's brow furrowed. "You haven't given yourself very much time to plan. We need to start making lists now and contacting suppliers if you don't want to miss out."

Quinn beamed at her. "And that leads me to my next thing. Will you be my maid of honor? I couldn't imagine anyone else helping with this wedding or being by my side for it. I mean, Beth is going to be a bridesmaid and Laura, too. But you're my best friend." Her eyes shimmered as she stared imploringly at Kelly.

Her throat squeezed shut, forcing Kelly to clear it, her eyes prickling. "Of course I will." Quinn gave her a quick hug. "After all, I wouldn't trust anyone else to make sure you get the wedding of your dreams."

"I've got so many ideas, and Jackson and I have already decided on a theme."

"Should I be scared?"

"Well, I know that it's not one that you're personally a fan of, but it's perfect for us." Kelly's eyes narrowed. *Don't tell me, it's—* "Christmas." *Okay then, looks like it is.* Two lines of worry appeared between Quinn's eyes. Kelly didn't understand why it meant so much to Quinn that she like her wedding theme. But if that was what she wanted, Kelly would give her the best dang Christmas wedding Colorado Springs had ever seen.

"I guess this calls for a bottle of Cristal." Kelly could almost see Quinn deflate in relief. "And then we can start making lists."

"I'll put my stuff away. You order the champagne, and then we can start."

Without waiting for her agreeance, Quinn dashed from the room. Kelly sat motionless for a moment before picking up the phone and dialing room service. She fought hard against the tears that she refused to let fall. *Get it together.* Quinn would never know how much it meant to Kelly that she'd asked her to be her maid of honor. Kelly wasn't like her. She didn't attract the love that Quinn did. But that didn't mean she didn't love the people she did let into her life, rather that she always felt insecure, as though they didn't care for the friendship as much as she did. Sniffing determinedly, she finished dialing.

Quinn fairly bounced back into the room, plonking several bridal magazines down on the coffee table. "I bought these so we can get some ideas."

Kelly leaned forward, straightening the magazines into an orderly pile. *Much better.* "Well, let's start with making a mood board for your theme." Kelly sat back, tapping away at her tablet, searching for images. "What do you think of these?" She held them out for her friend's inspection.

Quinn's mouth puckered as she pondered, grappling with what emotions the pictures evoked in her. "I like the color, but it feels kinda flat."

"Yeah, it needs more texture." She flicked to the next one. "How about this?"

Several hours and a couple bottles of champagne later, Kelly placed the tablet down in satisfaction. "I think we have a really good starting place for your theme. I'll start making some lists for information that I will need from you, and then I can shortlist some suppliers to contact." She stopped when Quinn began to giggle. "What?"

"You know you don't have to organize the wedding for me? I didn't ask you to be my maid of honor just so I could access your amazing event management skills. I asked you because you're my best friend."

A warm glow of acceptance flickered to life in the pit of

Kelly's stomach. "I know. I don't mean to be overbearing. I'll back off a bit."

Quinn patted her on the knee. "Oh, I'm going to need all the help I can get. I just don't want you to feel obligated to do it." She gave a little hiccup. "There is, however, one thing that is totally your responsibility to organize."

Kelly straightened, a sick feeling of apprehension that she'd forgotten something already shattering her. "What?"

"The hen's party."

Kelly's face split into a wide grin. "I'd be remiss in my duties if I didn't arrange that."

"Jackson might need some help with ideas for his, too. He wants to have it here in Vegas since that is where we met again."

"And all the best strippers are here, too."

"Kelly!" Her friend threw a pillow at her.

"Well, we both know that's true. I wonder if Thunder from Down Under will put in an exclusive appearance for your hens?" Kelly quickly made a mental note to get in touch with their manager. *Only the best for my bride.*

Quinn's cheeks flamed brightly. "Just remember that Jackson's sister and mom and probably grandmother if she gets her way will be there."

"That's okay. I bet Grandma Gregory would love looking at some prime examples of Aussie manhood."

"I can't believe you just said that!" Quinn gasped, her cheeks, if possible, growing even more scarlet. "Actually, I kinda can."

Kelly laughed, enjoying herself immensely. "Yeah, we both knew that was totally something I was going to say." She picked up her tablet again. "Now, let's talk guest list."

Much later, after a very tipsy Quinn had made her way to bed, Kelly sipped the last of her wine. The magazines that had been forgotten on the coffee table beckoned her and she picked one up, idly flicking through the pages. Happy brides and adoring grooms smiled at her from a variety of impossibly perfect settings. Proud, beaming mothers handed daughters bouquets of pristine flowers. A sadness that was so pure it robbed her of breath overcame her. The deepest, most secret part of her heart wept.

Things like that don't happen to women like me.

CHAPTER 5

Gleaming surfaces everywhere, so immaculate. Wyatt guiltily looked down to make sure he wasn't somehow trailing a line of dirt through the casino foyer. He could feel the stares of the people around them in their fancy clothes, eyeing the group that so obviously didn't belong in the same air space as them. *I wouldn't mind sharing some airspace with that little blonde over there.* The woman was leaning against the polished marble check in counter, her back to them, giving him an eyeful of her delightful curves. The way her form-fitting dress hugged her hips before it finished just above her shapely calves, the height of her heels exaggerating the length and line of her legs. *Okay, maybe there are some things worth coming to Vegas for.*

At the prompting of the staff member beside her, the woman slowly began to pivot. Anticipation stalled Wyatt's breathing, his muscles tensing. *Ah, heck no!*

"Jackson." Kelly glided toward them, all swishing hips and clicking heels and clearly basking in the appreciative stares directed at her.

"Kelly, what are you doing here?" Jackson stooped to give her a kiss on the cheek.

"Well, I know I wasn't able to get you guys a suite at The Chimera. Markus is still sulking about you taking his girl."

"She was never his girl," Jackson growled.

Kelly gave a light, breathy laugh. "I'm not sure he ever got that particular memo. Honestly, I'm amazed he let me use the High Roller Suite for us girls this weekend." She tilted her head sideways like some exotic bird. "Although I didn't really give him much of a choice." She smiled brightly up at Jackson. Wyatt, who was standing closest to him, felt himself smiling back, caught in the reflected warmth she sent to his friend. Her eyes narrowed suspiciously when she caught sight of it. Turning her body ever so slightly, she efficiently excluded Wyatt from the exchange. *Stuck up princess.*

"You still haven't told me why you're here," Jackson pressed.

"Well, I called in some favors. I can't have my bestie's fiancé slumming it in some cut-price room. I've organized for you to have one of the VIP rooms here." Kelly waved her hand imperiously and a short, very pretty man magically appeared at her side. *He's got smoother hands than Lisa from the beauty salon back home.* "This is Antonio, and he's the concierge here"—she beamed her thanks at Antonio—"and he's going to look after you for your stay. Just let him know of anything you need, and he'll arrange it for you." Kelly made a show of checking the time on the very expensive looking watch she wore. "Now, if you'll excuse me, I need to get back to my casino and work."

"Are you coming tonight for the group cocktails?" Jackson asked.

"Of course." She gave him a quick kiss on the cheek and, in a cloud of expensive smelling perfume, was gone.

Jackson picked up his bag, nodding at Antonio. "Thank you for letting us use your fancy room, I really appreciate it."

"For Kelly, anything. Now, if you'll follow me, I will show you your suite."

Wyatt lingered, breathing in the air where moments before Kelly had stood, the rest of the group making their way around him like water parting around a large pebble in its path. Jackson looked over his shoulder, his lips twitching.

"Are you coming, Wyatt, or are you just going to stand there daydreaming about pretty PR ladies?"

Wyatt had never wanted to punch his friend so much in his entire life. Grabbing his battered bag, he followed, satisfying himself with fantasizing about wiping that dumb smirk off his best friend's face.

EVERYTHING about her screamed expensive luxury. She had the look of a materialistic woman who loved to be pampered. *But dang, if Kelly didn't look good in that little black dress.*

Wyatt should have known that if Kelly was left in charge of organizing the cocktails, it was going to end up being held in a place like this. Black marble floors, black glass tables and fancy black sofas in tucked away corners, too low for a man to get himself comfortable on. All the waitresses drifting about looked like they were models in their spare time, and the uniforms they wore looked like something that had come straight from a magazine cover. Wyatt crossed and uncrossed his stretched-out legs. *Why isn't anything man-sized in this place?* Jackson was deep in conversation with Quinn's mom and sister-in-law. He grudgingly had to give it to Kelly. It had been a pretty cool surprise to have them show up unannounced.

Quinn waved her hands about animatedly as she talked to

Kelly on the other side of the room. Whatever she was saying obviously wasn't to Kelly's liking, her plump, pale pink mouth puckering like there wasn't enough sugar in her lemonade. Kelly looked guiltily in his direction, haughtily lifting her chin when she saw him staring at her. Wyatt dropped his eyes, embarrassed to have been caught. *I don't know why I was even looking at her.* It occurred to him that he was probably the topic of their conversation, given Kelly's reaction. What mystified him was why.

With a final surprisingly submissive nod to Quinn, she began to stroll through the crowd, nodding and saying a quick word to people she knew. A curious knot began to tighten in his stomach as she made her way torturously slowly toward him. She smiled, dimples dancing in her cheeks. *Has she always had them?*

"Are you having a good night?"

"It's different." He sipped the dregs of his warm beer.

"Can I get another one for you?" She gestured graciously at his glass, making him feel even more mulish.

"Not at the prices they charge here."

Kelly blinked at his venom. "You don't need to worry about that. I'm covering the bill."

Of course she is. "Princess, you must have more money than sense then."

Her perfect ivory skin mottled, outrage pouring from her blue-gray eyes. "Excuse me?"

"I mean, I can see how this is a place for you sort of people, but it's not for the normal folk like Jackson and me."

"Normal folk?"

"Yeah. The ones who understand the value of an honest dollar 'cause they have to work hard for every single penny that comes their way."

Perfectly arched pale gold brows furrowed, narrowed

eyes glaring icily at him. "What makes you think I don't work hard for my money?"

Wyatt leaned back into the too soft cushion of the ridiculous sofa. "Princess, you have the look of someone who was born into it."

Her nostrils flared and she stiffened. "You don't know anything about me."

"I know that you and Las Vegas have a lot in common."

"I told Quinn I would just be wasting my time being nice to you, and I was right."

He raised his now empty glass in salute. "Glad I didn't disappoint, princess."

"You know what's disappointing? The fact you couldn't even be bothered to get some new clothes for your best friend's bucks party. Instead you turn up in something that belongs in a thrift shop!" Spinning on her heel, she walked away with stiff dignity.

Wyatt raked his fingers through his hair. "I'll have you know, I did buy these new," he called out to her departing back. *It might have been ten years ago, but new is new.* He went to take another drink, frustrated to find it empty. No way was he going to put it on the princess's tab. With a groan, he crossed then uncrossed his arms. This friendly little joint cocktail soiree couldn't end fast enough for him, and then it would just be the boys. No princesses allowed. After all, isn't that what bucks parties are meant to be?

"Oh my," breathed Quinn, her eyes gratifyingly large as she rounded on Kelly. "You did all this for me?"

Kelly inspected her nails closely. "It's just a little something I threw together. Do you like it?"

"Yep. No one throws a party like you do," Quinn said. "I

know this was a little earlier than usual for a bachelorette party, but it's the only time everyone can get together before the wedding." Quinn's gaze was still sweeping the room, taking in Kelly's efforts.

"It wasn't a bother. You know me, I love a good party." And it was true. It was impossible to feel lonely or sad when one had a party to attend. It was one of the first things Kelly's mother had taught her.

Overall, it was rather nice to hear everyone ooh and aah. Mrs Williamson, Quinn's mom, had been the best, simply standing still, her hand to heart, taking it all in. Kelly had always had a soft spot for the dear woman. She suspected Quinn didn't appreciate just how great her mom was.

Kelly signaled to one of the handsome, brawny young men to bring her a drink. Sure, it was cliché, but she couldn't resist having the waiters only wearing tight trousers and bow ties. Sipping the signature Quinnsmo cocktail she'd had the resident mixologist create, she surveyed her handiwork. Pride of place was not one, but two fountains, each over six feet tall and flowing with one of Quinn's favorite things in the whole wide world—chocolate and Cristal. *Well, after Jackson these days.* The air was heavy with the mingled scent as the decadent liquids flowed. It looked like Quinn had already found them, judging by the glasses she held in each hand.

Beside the pool, Kelly had set up a pamper station offering manicures, facials, makeup and pedicures. Jackson's mom and sister were the first clients of that particular service. *Good on them. They seem like nice hardworking women. Maybe it will give them a taste for some self-care and luxury.*

And that wasn't even the best bit. Using all of her contacts, she'd managed to get swag bags laden with luxury items, some of which she was sure Quinn's guests could only have dreamed of, drooling over them in magazines. Every guest here was special to Quinn, and Quinn was special to Kelly. She'd pulled out all the stops to make this night memorable.

"Kelly, this is"—Quinn gestured at the setup— "amazing, even for you."

"Thank you, I try." Kelly tried to look humble but failed miserably, bursting out laughing. *Humble is never going to be my thing.*

"You didn't say how it went with Wyatt."

She thought about the black-haired rancher, that strong jawline mulishly thrusting out as he'd hauled insults at her and 'her kind of people.' Anger for the undeserved verbal attack left a bitter taste in her mouth, one even the Quinnsmo failed to wash away. *It's not like he's the first man to ever judge me without bothering to get to know me.* "He's never going to be one of my favorite people."

"I know you two didn't get off to the best start. A little bit of that is on you, Kelly."

She squirmed under Quinn's direct gaze. "Yeah, well, how was I meant to know he wasn't the driver?"

Quinn laughed, the peals of laughter rippling from her. "Lots of people wouldn't have assumed he was the driver."

"The man is such a pain and he's so tight with his money. Did you see what he was wearing?" Kelly expertly deflected.

"I saw a hardworking man who doesn't live an extravagant life." *Why was Quinn defending him?*

"Well, the man needs to live a little. Maybe tonight will make him loosen up." Kelly smiled smugly into her glass, enjoying the thought of the mischief she'd arranged.

Quinn's eyes narrowed over the rim of her own glass filled with thick liquid chocolate. "What have you done, Kelly?"

"Nothing. Much." A group of large, burly men trooping into the suite thankfully cut off that line of questioning. Kelly had never been so thankful to see male strippers in her life. She giggled as Grandma Gregory got settled into position, prime and center. *Go, Grandma. At least she knows how to have some fun.*

Quinn wasn't so easily distracted by the hotness that was the man flesh of Thunder from Down Under. "He's Jackson's best friend and also his best man. You both need to play nice."

Kelly poked her tongue out. "Yeah, well, tell him that." And with a little flounce she went and sat next to Grandma G.

~

"I MEAN, can you believe her? She's the most materialistic person I've ever met. Not to mention spoiled and rude." Wyatt drained his beer in a single agitated gulp, wiping his mouth with the back of his hand.

"Don't you think you're being a bit harsh? Quinn said she asked Kelly to go over and try to mend fences. She did try, didn't she?" Jackson's left brow raised slightly.

Guilt settled uncomfortably in his gut. Or maybe it was the beer he'd just chugged. *Anyway, why is Jackson defending her?* "I might not have given her a chance," he admitted grudgingly, looking around at the opulent suite Kelly had arranged for them—not that there was anything wrong with the room and catering he'd booked. *Typical that she'd take control over something she had no right to.* He was pretty sure his entire house would fit in the main living space. A bar had been set up on the terrace offering twelve different craft beers on tap and a selection of spirits. Enormous TV screens had been set up broadcasting different sports and there were waitresses wandering around carrying trays with buffalo wings, ribs and other manly type snacks. As much as the admission riled him, he had to give it to Kelly. She'd set up the space just right.

"Look, I know she was a bit high maintenance when you met." Jackson snagged a mozzarella stick as a waitress went past. "But her and Quinn are tight. I can guarantee you're going to be seeing her around at family events for years, not just this wedding. Anyway, she's Quinn's maid of honor. And from what my beautiful fiancée explained to me, there's stuff that you guys need to do together for the wedding." He bit into the cheesy morsel with relish. "These may be the best mozzarella sticks I've ever had."

"I hear there have been some naughty boys who need to be shown the full force of the law." Two female police officers walked in, handcuffs swinging from one's fingertips.

"At last," Jackson's grandpa muttered. "I was beginning to think you hadn't arranged any entertainment."

"I didn't." Wyatt hadn't thought Jackson would be interested in scantily clad buxom ladies.

"Well, I'm sure as heck glad someone did. Do you have any dollar bills?"

"Grandpa!" Jackson's shocked laughter rang out.

"What? I'm old, not dead. Don't bother. I'll go see if your father has any." Muttering, the old man walked off.

"I'm waiting," the police offer demanded, her companion slapping the baton she carried against an open palm. "And you don't want to see me angry."

Levi, Jackson's brother-in-law, and his father dragged him forward, Jackson laughingly resisting. It goaded Wyatt that the entertainment was so obviously welcomed by everyone. *One more reason to dislike the interfering blonde princess.*

CHAPTER 6

The stunning slender trees were in the midst of their leaf-changing splendor. Not only the Aspen trees that lined the street, but further in the distance on the mountains, bright bursts of color between the cool green of the pines. Kelly stooped to pick up a brilliant gold leaf that cartwheeled into her path on a gust of chilly wind. She marveled at the translucent yellow that crunched beneath her hand. Another gust made her pull her coat tighter around her, the promise of winter in the air.

"Thanks for coming. I know you've got a lot on with the finishing touches for the new act to bump in." The tip of Quinn's nose was beginning to redden from the chill.

"Actually, it's nice to get away from all that crazy once in a while. But if you ever tell anyone I said that, I'll deny it till the day I die." Kelly wagged her finger, her features severe. Quinn wasn't the least bit intimidated, her laughter sending gusts of steam wafting out. *Like some sort of dragon.* Kelly tried to look tougher, only managing to increase her friend's mirth. *If dragons giggled.*

"No one would believe me even if I did tell." Quinn wiped tears from her eyes. *I'm not sure it was that funny.* She blew as she rubbed her hands together, giving a shiver. "Now, let's head over to a coffee shop I know and get a nice cup of hot cocoa with marshmallows." Her eyes glowed with anticipation.

"Only if they put bourbon in it."

"I'm pretty sure that's how Grandma Gregory makes hers," Quinn retorted mischievously.

"I knew there was a reason I liked her. My gosh, I nearly split my sides when she jumped on that dancer's lap in Vegas." Actually, Kelly wasn't sure who enjoyed themselves more—Grandma Gregory or the dancer.

"They're really good people here, Kelly. Hopefully you'll keep visiting me and get to know them all." Quinn bit her lip, looking like there was more she wanted to say.

Kelly had her suspicions. "Out with it."

"I don't know what you mean." Quinn's eyes widened, guilelessly shining back at her.

"If you're going to tag something on about Wyatt, I'm going to save you the trouble and stop you right there. I have no interest in discussing him on a cold street when I could be sitting somewhere toasty having a cappuccino and planning your wedding."

"Fine, but I'm not giving up." Quinn began to walk, her determined steps quickly eating up the sidewalk.

"I wouldn't expect you to."

Quinn pushed open a door decorated in Halloween skulls, spiders and cobwebs. This town sure did like to get in the spirit of things. Inside there were more spooky décor and little carved pumpkins amongst the glass cookie jars on the counter. Everything smelled of cinnamon and nutmeg, but Kelly was just grateful that it was lovely and warm inside.

Her friend fairly skipped up to the counter and, judging from the familiar greetings, she was a regular here.

"Do you want your usual?" the girl behind the register asked, her pen poised above the cardboard cup in readiness.

"Yes, please, and a slice of your heavenly pumpkin pie." Kelly couldn't be sure, but it looked like a little drool was pooling on the side of Quinn's mouth. "And my friend will want something, too." She turned expectantly and looked at Kelly with raised brows.

"I'll get a chai cappuccino, please, and a slice of the pumpkin pie. It must be good if Quinn picks it over something chocolate." Kelly couldn't resist a teasing wink to the girl.

"I'll get these done and bring them straight over," she promised, writing on the cups.

Quinn directed them to a spotlessly clean table set in front of the bright window overlooking the street. Kelly had to give it to her friend. She'd found a great local coffeehouse to hang out in. She moved the sugar shaker to one side and took out her tablet. "Now, have you decided where you want to hold the ceremony and reception?"

"In the old red barn."

"Really? Won't it be a bit cold in there at Christmas?" Kelly's finger hovered over the screen, surprise making her look up.

"That's what Wyatt said, too. But Jackson and Grandpa both reckon they can find a way to heat it up." Quinn paused to smile at the waitress as their pies and warm drinks were set in front of them. "It's really important to me that it's held there."

And Kelly knew Quinn could be like a dog with a bone once she'd set her mind to something. "Okay, I'll make it work. How about the reception?"

"It's going to be there, too." Quinn scooped a forkful of the pie and leisurely sampled it, her eyes half-closed in ecstasy.

Kelly pursed her mouth. It did have potential and a lot of space to play with. "I'll need to measure it, of course."

"Of course." Quinn mumbled around her dessert.

Kelly picked up her fork. The pie did look delicious. "Now, for the really important stuff. Pie!"

MUTTERING and shuffling noises came from inside the barn as Wyatt thrust his hands deep into his pockets. *It was almost glove weather.* Quinn had told him she'd thought Jackson was somewhere working with his father, but she wasn't sure where exactly. He had to give it to his friend. Jackson had picked a real sweetheart there. It made a man wonder what it might be like to come home to a woman like that. He brusquely pushed the thought from his mind. *Ain't got time for that sort of nonsense.* The sad fact of the matter was that none of the women around here had held his interest for more than a fleeting second. But that wasn't to say they'd stopped offering.

The door swung easily on its recently oiled hinges with not a sound of protest as it swung wide. It took a moment for his eyes to adjust to the dim lighting inside. When they did, he found himself confronted with a glaring pale blonde beauty, measuring tape and notebook in hand, and sitting at her feet staring adoringly up at her was Jackson's dog, Nitro.

"You know they have lights, right?" he couldn't resist saying.

"Of course I do. It was lit up for Quinn's party," snapped Kelly, a becoming pink blossoming on her cheeks. *Like roses against snow.* Wyatt caught himself and wondered where on earth that poetic nonsense was coming from.

"Then why are you standing in the dark, princess?" He rested a shoulder and hip against the doorway, still not having fully entered.

"I couldn't find the switch." She tossed her hair across her shoulders in defiance. The cobwebs in them only slightly marring the proud gesture. "And Nitro hasn't been any help in locating them. In fact, all he does is trip me up."

For a woman with such a cool outside, she certainly fired up nicely. Made him wonder if he could thaw out her iciness to find the warm woman inside. Wyatt blinked. *Where had that thought come from?* If Kelly was starting to seem tempting, he really needed to get more female company. He reached over and flicked on the lights, bathing the dusty barn in a golden glow. Kelly was dressed in jeans and a sweater with a puffer jacket. It was probably the most normal outfit he'd ever seen her wear and dang it if she didn't look amazing in it.

"What are you doing here anyway?"

"Quinn wants to hold the ceremony and reception here. I'm measuring everything up to see what needs to be done to make the space work, but it's going to need a lot of effort to get it into shape." She set the end of her tape measure on a stall wall and began to walk away from it slowly, the tape stretching taut.

Wyatt bristled at her implication. "It was good enough for her birthday. You didn't have any complaints then."

He swallowed his irritation as she heaved a sigh. "A birthday party has very different requirements to a formal wedding ceremony and separate reception for one hundred guests." Kelly spoke slowly and clearly like she was speaking to an imbecile.

Wyatt gritted his teeth, irked at her patronizing tone. He was somewhat mollified when the end of her tape measure came loose and retracted back into its case. Wyatt didn't even attempt to hide his laughter, but he was a little shocked by her very unladylike cussing. *Well, well, Kelly. Not such a princess after all.*

He strode forward, appreciating her ramrod straight back as she marched to return the vexing measurer back in place. "Here, I'll hold it. Wouldn't want you to break a nail or something."

From the icy glare she directed at him, it was clear she wasn't amused. "I can manage."

"Yeah, you really can't. It will get done quicker if you let me help you." Wyatt's voice may have been soft, but there was a quiet command to his words. She handed the end to him and, without replying, began to step backwards again. *Watching the way she got her panties all in a bunch, well, it was almost becoming an addiction.*

"Thank you. That was the last measurement I needed anyway." *Was she dismissing him?*

"So, what are your ideas for this wedding anyway?" Kelly stared at him, her huge, blue-gray eyes indecipherable. It was almost as though she was trying to decide if he seriously wanted to know or just wanted another opportunity to mock her. *Which is kinda fair. Heck, I don't even know which it is most of the time.* As she continued to mull it over, Wyatt surprised himself with a genuine curiosity to see what she had planned. "Come on. Pretty please?" He held out his hand.

Eyes narrowed, she walked across to a stall wall where she'd set her bag down and retrieved her tablet. Swiping on it, she gracefully made her way over to him. "I don't have ideas for just any old wedding. My ideas are for this one." She handed it over.

Wyatt found himself looking at a selection of images, all white with tiny hints of gold as the only other color. And the setting was so stiff and formal, cold and impersonal. One image had the snowy white aisle lined with what looked to be white spray-painted lifeless tree trunks, their pale slender limbs stretching up to the ceiling. The table settings were all white with crystal centerpieces set on mirrored circles.

"I think you might want to rethink your theme."

Pink crept up her neck as her mouth hardened. "Excuse me?"

"This wedding here"—he pointed down at the tablet —"isn't for Quinn or Jackson. It's nothing like their tastes. You're planning a wedding that would suit you."

"I am not," Kelly huffed, eyes spitting fire." "I know Quinn a lot better than you do, and this is what she asked for. A Christmas theme."

"Yeah, but a Christmas theme that suits Quinn. She's funny and sweet and loves Christmas. So, if she wants Christmas, give her Christmas and everything it means. Not some sort of snow queen's wedding for someone like you." A flicker of hurt—no, surely, he was wrong—flashed in her wide eyes before she blinked it away.

"Someone like me?" Her tone was frigid. "I think it's classy and beautiful." *Just like you.* Wyatt was growing heartily sick of these thoughts sneaking into his brain. Her next words drove any admiration away. "But what would you know about that?" Her lips curled in derision. "I mean, look at the heap of junk you drive. Do you even have a job?"

"Princess, you don't know the first thing about me."

Wyatt spun on his booted heel and stomped out of the barn. He knew he was the one to blame for the loathing threaded through each word she'd spat at him, but she seemed to bring the worse out of him with her high-handed, uppity manner. *Why do I act this way around her? Grandpa didn't raise me to talk to a lady like this.* Wyatt's door screeched alarmingly as he yanked it open, only adding to his dark mood. *Heck, I don't mean to say half the mean things I say to her.* Guilt made him grip the steering wheel tightly, its cold leaden weight settling in his stomach. *I need to try harder with her, if only for Quinn and Jackson.*

CHAPTER 7

*I*n Kelly's line of work, she'd met all kinds of celebrities, wannabes, nevergonnabes, washed-up has-beens and, once in a while, actual superstars. And not just any superstar, but Nashville Royalty. Presley Barnett was just about the hottest thing in country music and had been since she'd strutted onto a stage singing her own songs at the age of sixteen. It really shouldn't have surprised anyone that it would be the career path she would take, since her daddy played drums for The King and her mama had been a famous country singer in her own right. It wasn't often that Kelly got starstruck, but if it was going to happen, it would be at this meeting.

Unusually, this time Kelly had been the one being told where the meeting would be held, and she was slightly shocked to discover that it would be at a local barbeque joint off the strip. Stepping up to the front of house hostess, she smiled, the smell of hickory and mesquite heavy in the air.

"Are you able to show me where Miss Barnett is?"

"I'm sorry, we don't have anyone here with that name."

Kelly removed her oversized sunglasses to fix her with a

steady gaze, the hostess dropping her eyes first. "Miss Barnett is expecting me."

"Let me go check."

"Do that." Kelly stowed her shades safely in her handbag, checking her phone discreetly for any messages.

"If you'd like to come with me," the hostess said, leading her to a table that was slightly more private than the rest. Though it was partly shielded, it was still much more accessible to the public than a lot of the talent Kelly had worked with over the years would have accepted.

Two women, easily identifiable as being mother and daughter by their obvious resemblance, looked up at their approach. "Mrs Barnett, Miss Barnett, I'm Kelly Hutchinson." Kelly smiled and held her hand out.

The younger one stood to her feet quickly to return the handshake, her deep chestnut hair glossy under the overhead light. "Makes me feel like a schoolteacher being called that. Please, call me Presley." Her voice was like molasses on a warm day.

The older woman, her face only slightly wrinkled and her hair still as thick and glossy as her daughter's but who Kelly knew for a fact was in her sixties, smiled with shrewd eyes. She was the one who had to be gotten onside if any deals were going to be made. "Pleased to meet you, Kelly. Are you fixin' to be standing there all day? Pull up a pew."

"Thank you, I will." Kelly settled herself quickly, feeling like she'd already lost control of the meeting.

Mrs Barnett waved for the waiter and, with a fearful look leaving Kelly wondering if he'd had dealings with the older woman before, he quickly trotted over. "Can I get you ladies anything?"

"I would like some baby back ribs and tea," Mrs Barnett instructed.

"Would you like cream or lemon with that?"

"Oh Lord, don't get her started," Presley muttered. But it was too late. The damage was already done.

Mrs Barnett's hand flew to her heart in shocked horror. "Suga, if I ask for tea, best be thinking I'm asking for sweet tea."

"Yes, ma'am," the waiter hastily agreed, turning to Presley. "And you, miss?"

"I'll have a Bloody Mary and some hot chicken." Presley arched a perfectly shaped brow in Kelly's direction. "What are you fixin' to get?"

"I'm fine. I ate before I came." Kelly stalled, not wanting to admit her aversion to spicy food.

"You came to a meeting with two southern ladies at a barbeque restaurant and ate before you came?" Mrs Barnett's brows were so high they were liable to touch the rafters.

"I never know what to expect when meeting clients for the first time." Kelly was so far on the back foot she was lucky she wasn't in reverse.

"Get the girl a Bloody Mary and some smoked mac and cheese," Mrs Barnett commanded, a pleased expression crossing her face as she watched the waiter scuttle away. "You look like you could stand to have a little more meat on your bones."

"You'll have to excuse Mama. She is used to telling everyone what to do—myself included." Presley winked at Kelly.

Kelly found herself warming to the country singer. There was just something so genuine and engaging about her. As far as she could tell, she didn't seem to be suffering from an excess of ego.

"Someone has to be the captain of this ship," her mother retorted, fiddling with the necklace she wore at her throat. "I hear that Cooper Mason won't be filling a spot next year?"

Wow, word sure did get around fast! "No, his agent seemed

to believe that Mr Cooper had more star power than he has now in the Autumn of his career. I wasn't about to agree to the outrageous demands they presented me with." Kelly looked Mrs Barnett directly in the eye, the warning clear. *I'm not afraid to play hardball when I have to, lady.*

"I think ya'll find that Presley certainly doesn't lack in the star department."

"I couldn't agree more, and The Chimera would welcome the opportunity to provide her with a residency." Kelly poured herself a glass of water, carefully setting the bottle back on the table. "As long as we can agree on terms."

"I'm sure you'll find our terms more than fair." Mrs Barnett's eyes began to sparkle, a glow of anticipation filling them. This was a woman after Kelly's own heart, finding the thrill of negotiation intoxicating.

"Mama, Kelly," Presley began, waiting as the waiter settled their drinks down in front of them. Kelly smiled when she noticed that Mrs Barnett's drink was last, and the waiter was already moving away from the table before the glass had touched the surface. "I think I'd like to hear what you can offer me as far as supporting me in providing the best performance experience I can for my fans." She raised her glass, the end of the straw poised against her blush-colored lips. "If I'm happy with that, then you two can battle out the details. Deal?"

"Deal." Kelly liked this country singer a great deal. She only prayed that her negotiation skills were equal to the mother's.

"AND THEN TOLD me that I needed to provide a beehive on the roof of The Chimera so her daughter could have a spoonful of the freshly harvested honey each night before she performed." Kelly rolled her eyes dramatically.

"Oh, wow. Where on earth am I going to source a beehive?" Quinn bit down on her lip anxiously.

"You don't. Presley set her mother straight and said that, as long as it's organic, unprocessed honey will do. She even said that we should be able to get some from a health store."

"Presley seems nice."

Kelly sipped her red wine, glad that another day was over. It was nice to catch up with Quinn on the nights she was in town and just have girl time. "She really is, but I wouldn't want to cross her. Underneath all that southern country charm, I think she could be brutal if you did wrong by her."

"I'll try to remember that. You know who else is nice? Wyatt." Guileless hazel eyes returned Kelly's suddenly stormy stare.

"Yeah, well, I haven't really seen that side of him. And he doesn't take any pride in himself." *Maybe if he brushed his hair once in a while or wore better clothes, he'd actually look half decent.* A funny fluttering started in her stomach as she thought about his black curls and arresting blue eyes. Angry with herself, she glared at Quinn. "I mean, does he even have a job?"

"Of course he does. Whatever gave you the idea he didn't?" Kelly didn't really appreciate the way Quinn looked at her like she was simple.

"The state of the truck he drives, his clothes, I don't know everything about him"—Kelly ticked each item off on her fingers—"and when I did ask him what he did for a job, he didn't say anything." She tried not to let too much of her triumphant smugness show.

"Did you ask when the two of you were fighting?" Did Quinn have to give her such a longsuffering look? *It's not my fault Wyatt is always so disagreeable to be around.* "Actually, don't answer that. When aren't the two of you arguing?"

"Hey, I don't start it. Well, not all the time."

"No, you don't. But you also don't help either." Quinn seemed to be considering what to say next. "Look, I don't know why Wyatt didn't say anything when you asked him about what he did. It's probably because he's just a stubborn as you."

"Hey!" Kelly didn't like what her friend was implying. "I have nothing in common with that country bumpkin."

Quinn rolled her eyes. "Anyway, google Hope Springs Horse Rescue, and then let me know if you still think Wyatt doesn't have a job or why he drives the truck he does."

Kelly sniffed. "Maybe, but I'd much rather talk about what style of wedding dress you think you might try on this weekend when I come down. It's going to be so exciting."

"So, you're still fine to come down then? I wish Mom could come over, but there's no way she could afford two trips so close together." Quinn's eyes misted and she blinked.

"I wouldn't miss it for the world." Kelly had an idea and, at the very least, it would mean she wouldn't be thinking about Wyatt. It was becoming a joke how he always seemed to enter her thoughts. It was beyond annoying, and it was going to stop right now.

KELLY TYPED Hope Springs Horse Rescue into the search bar of her tablet. Several results flashed up, and she clicked on one. She scanned the welcome information. *Hope Springs Horse Rescue takes horses in need and rehabilitates them. Owner Wyatt Daniels—wait, what?* She quickly read it again. Maybe it was possible there was another Wyatt Daniels who lived in

Colorado Springs and owned the horse rescue Quinn had expressly told her to google. *Oh, come on. Who am I kidding?*

Several hours later, Kelly had read heartbreaking stories of cases of abuse or neglect and the happy endings for some that were able to be made healthy again, even if to just live their days out on the ranch, or the gut-wrenching sad endings where she prayed they had spent their last moments knowing they were safe and cared for. At times, she had to blink tears away as the screen blurred. All those times Wyatt had been sour about money and how frivolous her spending was and that of those he deemed to be the same as her, it had been because this is what he spent his on.

But it was more than that. Reading the stories of terrified, malnourished horses and seeing them, their eyes calm and soft as they stood with Wyatt or, in some cases, with him sitting on their backs, it was clear that he gave more than cash to these animals. He gave them his all.

A light quivery sensation of guilt settled in her stomach. She might have misjudged Wyatt. But she refused to take the entire blame, especially for their first meeting. At any time, he could have cleared it up. But instead, he'd let her act the fool. Still, looking at what he did with his life, maybe all the comments about his truck and him being poor, they might have been a bit much. She stiffened, momentarily abashed. She was going to have to eat a lot of crow to make this right, but never let it be said that Kelly Hutchinson wasn't able to admit it when she was wrong.

Draining the last of her wine, she rinsed the glass under the tap in the kitchen sink. Images of a wide smile set full of gleaming white teeth in a tanned face popped into her head. *Maybe it was okay to dream about him after all.*

CHAPTER 8

The ladies gathered together on the cream sofa lined up for their viewing comfort like little birds perched on a powerline. They waited with their hands clutching the stems of their champagne glasses so tightly in anticipation that Kelly feared for the crystal's safety. Several mannequins were positioned around the room, swathed in luxurious fabrics and diamantes. The sales attendant slipped through the white and gold damask drapes, pausing, gauging the exact moment all eyes were on her and, with a dramatic swish, pulled the curtain back. Slowly, as if unsure how to maneuver in her voluminous skirts, Quinn emerged like a butterfly out of a chrysalis.

A collective gasp of indrawn breath greeted the sight of the glowing bride-to-be in all her wedding dress splendor. "Are you all quiet because you like it or…?" Quinn's voice trailed off, a tentative smile ghosting her lips as her eyes darted from face to face.

Kelly raised her glass in salute to the vision in front of her. The off-the-shoulder dress was the softest shade of cream, a delicate lace overlay covering the bodice, extending down to her slender wrists. The plentiful satin skirts were overlaid with a multitude of chiffon, giving her the appearance of a real-life princess. The icing on the cake was a wide scarlet ribbon that encircled her waist before gathering in a large diamante-accented bow behind her, the long, wide tails trailing down to finish several inches before the end of her train.

"You're beautiful."

Quinn's eyes began to mist as she looked at the women who had gathered to see her dress as well as pick out bridesmaid dresses. Besides Kelly, Grandma Gregory, Hannah, Beth and Laura had all come as well. Quinn looked at her soon-to-be husband's family, smiling her thanks. "It means a lot to me to have you all here. I just wish Mom had of been able to make it."

Hannah, Quinn's soon-to-be mother-in-law, handed her a tissue to blot at her tears. "Aw, honey, I understand, but I'm honored to fill in today." Quinn gave her a watery smile.

Kelly drained her glass. *Dang it, I'm not going to let my bestie miss her mom on a day like this.* She began rummaging around in her handbag. "I've got an idea," she said, holding her phone triumphantly aloft.

Quinn gave her a quizzical look as her friend rapidly began to tap away on her phone. "Hello?" A familiar voice made Quinn's bottom lip tremble.

"Mrs Williamson, hang on, I'm just going to turn you around so you can see how beautiful your daughter looks." Kelly turned her phone to reveal Quinn's mother peering out from the screen.

"Mom!" Quinn cried. "I can't believe I didn't think to do a video call. I feel like a real goose now, getting all upset because you aren't here."

"Aw, Quinn, you look so beautiful. I can't believe that my little baby girl is standing there in a wedding dress."

"I think I'm going to cry," Hannah whispered to Grandma. The attendant discreetly passed a tissue to her.

"Best leave the box," Grandma commanded, reaching for one herself.

Kelly remained holding the phone steady for her best friend, an insistent twinge tugging at her heart. Quinn was marrying into a family who was welcoming her with open arms. And not just that, but she still had her own loving family. An empty hollowness threatened to overwhelm Kelly. She was alone. By now, she should be used to it. But why did it suddenly seem like a burden she could no longer carry?

Quinn gave another twirl at her mother's urging. "Are you going to be cold in it?" Mrs Williamson always was practical.

"I think we can add a sort of capelet thing and then she can take it off once she's safely in the warmth of the barn," Kelly said. Quinn smiled gratefully at her, obviously not having thought of it herself.

"I have to go, Quinn, but you look beautiful, and Dad and I love you lots and lots. It's not long now till we're there and we can see it in the flesh."

Quinn looked like she was fogging up again. "I'll take some pics for you," Kelly quickly offered.

"That would be lovely, Kelly. I know our little girl will have a fantastic wedding with you helping her." Kelly found herself standing a little taller at the older woman's words. Such a small thing to say, and she bet Mrs Williamson would never know how much it meant to her.

"I'll make sure of it," she promised.

"Bye, Mom. I love you. See you soon." Quinn sniffled as the screen went blank.

"Okay, now, have you thought about other elements you want to use to tie in your Christmas theme?" Kelly had heard that when toddlers cried, it was best to distract them with something shiny. Maybe it also worked with brides-to-be.

Quinn blinked, jerked out of wallowing in self-pity, obviously thrown off by the change in topic. "Um, well, I had the red ribbon added to this dress." She gently laid her palms on her stomach. "I didn't want to look too cartoonish."

Kelly appraised it with a practiced eye. "And it's lovely and definitely a step in the right direction."

"How 'bout we add some of those mini pinecones to her flowers?" Grandma suggested, holding her index finger and thumb an inch apart.

"Oh, and maybe some holly berries?" Hannah added.

"I think sprigs of fir needles would look lovely and they would give her bouquet the most marvelous Christmas smell," Beth said, leaning forward to join the conversation.

"I think you girls might be onto something." Kelly pursed her mouth. "We can continue that with the rest of the decorations." She touched her friend gently on the hand. "I think we can give you a Christmas wedding that's exactly right for you." *Not a snow queen.* "Now, are we going to start trying on some of these bridesmaids' dresses?"

Quinn's eyes sparkled as she clapped her hands together excitedly. "Oh my gosh, yes. I have narrowed it down to three different colors."

Beth's eyes narrowed, her hands creeping to her generous hips. "Isn't it usual to agree on a style first and then order it in a color that suits?"

Quinn looked like she was about to explode, her smile stretching wide to expose her teeth, her tightly fisted hands going to her mouth. "So, I came up with the best idea. I don't want you all in the same style." She looked from Kelly's slender shorter form to Beth's curvier taller frame and then to Laura's adolescent body. "I want each of you to have a dress that makes you feel magical. It's a Christmas-themed wedding, being held on Christmas Eve. I want all of that happiness and excitement and yes, Christmas spirit to shine out." Her voice rang with conviction. *I wonder if she'll let me wear a bikini and maybe walk down the aisle holding a colorful cocktail. That's my usual Christmas spirit.*

"And we're going to start with"—she slowly waved her finger between her three bridesmaids—"you, Kelly."

"So, my Christmas spirit is more Bora Bora than Colorado Ranch." Kelly scrunched up her face, letting her words end in an unspoken question.

"Well, you're going to have to find a little bit more Christmas spirit than you usually have." Quinn planted her hands on her hips, her expression brooking no disobedience. *I'd say that's a no to the bikini then.*

"Yes, ma'am."

Quinn patted her happily on the cheek. "Come with me. I have some ideas."

Kelly wasn't sure if that was meant to make her feel reassured or terrified. Deciding it was better for all concerned if she was obedient rather than defiant, she meekly followed the bride-to-be into the dressing room. *Colorado Ranch Christmas spirit, here I come.*

THE CRUNCH of tires on gravel sounded outside the barn. Wyatt gave the emancipated Clydesdale a soothing rub on the forehead. "Don't worry, big fella. That sounds like the vet, and he's going to make you feel a lot better." He hastened out to help Doc Bryan bring in his equipment, stopping dead at the sight of the unfamiliar micro car parked there. *What the heck?* His mouth gaped open as a horribly familiar small blonde stepped out, pulling a woolen cap snuggly down about her ears.

"You're going to catch flies if you stay like that," Kelly said tartly as she made her way over to him.

"Look, I don't know why you're here, but I don't have time for whatever it is. How did you even find out where I live?" Confusion made his thoughts all muddled. He absolutely hated feeling unprepared.

"If you don't want people turning up on your doorstep, best not be putting your address up on the internet." She pulled red gloves on. Somehow Wyatt had known without ever having given it much thought that she would favor red. It was classy in the same way black was, but it had an edge to it—a hint that maybe a bit of a rebel lurked beneath her cool exterior. "I hired that itty-bitty car and drove all the way out here to see what you do."

Wyatt stared at her. *Who the heck was this woman? There was no way Kelly Hutchinson would use a word like itty-bitty.* "It is a little on the small side."

Her pale pink lips curved. "I think you're being generous."

The beginnings of a smile tipped the corners of his mouth in answer to hers before he could think to do anything else. But still, he was wary of this new Kelly. "Why do you want to see what I do?"

"Why didn't you tell me this was what you did when I asked if you had a job?" She raised a pale gold arched brow at him.

He jammed his hands deep into the pockets of his jeans. "I guess because it was so obvious that you'd already made your mind up about me."

Kelly bit her lip, looking away, but not before he caught a flicker of guilt in her eyes. He blinked, not sure he'd read her expression correctly. The Kelly he'd had the displeasure of getting to know the last several months sure as heck didn't suffer from guilt. "I'm sorry about that, and you do deserve an apology. I might not have been the most—" She waved a hand in the air.

"Nicest?" he supplied.

"Let's split the difference and say gracious." Irritated eyes narrowed dangerously. "Is there anything you would like to say to me?"

"I accept your apology."

Pale brows shot skyward. "I beg your pardon. That's it?"

"And if you're still interested, I'll show you around, but only quickly. I'm expecting someone." Wyatt smiled magnanimously down at her.

He couldn't be sure, but based on her rapidly reddening complexion, any minute now he half-expected steam to come out of her ears like a cartoon character. Kelly muttered under her breath. Some of the words Wyatt managed to catch he wasn't even sure what they meant, but he was certain it was some sort of threat to the continued well-being of his person.

Deciding it was best to ignore it, he began to lead her around the outside of the barn to where rugged horses grazed in fields and yards of various sizes. Overhead the clouds were heavy, a promise of snow in the air. "I try to give all the horses time turned out. Some of the worser cases will spend weeks in the stalls until they are in a stable enough condition for them to have some outside time. Even then, it will be restricted to a small yard."

"You keep them in to let them settle?" Kelly asked, a soft glow of confusion on her face.

"We quarantine all horses as soon as they arrive on the property and arrange a vet to go over them to let me know exactly what I'm dealing with health wise. Most of them have heavy worm burdens and will get an initial drench then if they are able to. If they have been abused, there are usually wounds that need to be treated. Or if they are malnourished,

I have to give them multiple small feeds throughout the day because their stomachs can't handle too much. I also need to gain their trust in a safe environment."

"I can't imagine how traumatized they are." She looked out over the horses. Wyatt tried to see what she was seeing. The horses were all rugged up against the cooler weather. Most were old or still recovering. Some were in patched canvas rugs, old and well-used, but still in a sturdy condition. He would need to purchase more next winter, but for now they were still able to do the job. The fencing was in a good safe condition—that was something he would never scrimp on. Wyatt prided himself on the safety he provided the animals he was responsible for.

"I don't know that I could trust again after some of the things these animals have gone through. In fact, I have a new horse that arrived yesterday in the barn," Wyatt responded matter-of-factly.

"Is that the one you're waiting for the vet for?" There was a pensive shimmer in the shadow of her eyes.

"Yeah." He still didn't entirely trust this new, softer side of Kelly. But what the heck? "Do you want to come in and meet him?"

"I'd love to. Unless you think I would stress him?"

Her softly concerned words made his heart do a funny flip flop. *Dang, who was this girl?* A white snowflake fluttered between them. Her eyes grew enormous, following its graceful descent to the ground, rocketing back up to meet his.

"Is that what I think it is?"

Wyatt gave a nonchalant shrug. "If you're thinking it's snow, then yeah." Another fell between them. She gave a delighted girlish squeal, lifting her face to the sky, letting the snowflakes softly fall on her pale, delicate skin. He'd always thought there was a certain kind of magic to the first snow of the season. Now, staring at her mesmerized, he felt like a man drowning.

"I've never been snowed on before." Snowflakes clung to her eyelashes, framing eyes the color of a wintery sky.

"For a girl who has everything, you seem to have missed some of the most priceless things you can experience." Wyatt snapped his mouth shut, his gaze sliding away from hers when he noticed her staring at him, her expression unfathomable. "Do you want to meet Maximus or not?" he said gruffly.

"Is that the name of the horse? Maximus?" Sweet relief flooded him that his ungracious words hadn't wrecked the fragile truce between them.

"Yeah."

"Lead the way," she commanded, for all the world sounding like a little general.

He marched into the barn, uncomfortably aware of how judgmental she had been of Jackson's barn—a barn that was in a much better condition than the one she was now standing in. Wyatt stopped and stood quietly, giving the horse inside the opportunity to decide for himself if he wanted to come closer. He was impressed when Kelly calmly followed his lead, peeking at the horse inside from the corner of her eye.

"Oh my, he looks like a big one." *Possibly the understatement of the year.*

"He's a Clydesdale and standing at 16.3 hands high."

From inside the stall, slow breaths sounded as if trying to smell if this new human meant to harm him. One tentative step torturously slow after another, the horse inside shuffled closer until a large heavily whiskered muzzle slowly extended, nostrils quivering.

"Hello, Maximus," Kelly breathed. "What do I do?" she asked Wyatt.

"Just stand there. Let him smell you. Keep talking slow and steady." Wyatt was surprised that Maximus had engaged with her.

"Hey, big boy. Look at that gorgeous mustache you have. I didn't know horses had them."

"Clydesdales are known for them." Wyatt slowly rested his hip against the stall wall. "Maximus has some of the best bloodlines you'll find in the country. But somewhere along the line, he'd fallen into the wrong hands, gotten a reputation as being difficult, and then was put out into a barren paddock and forgotten." Disgust at his own kind filled his voice, making it gravelly.

"Do you think he'll let me touch him?"

"We can only try. Let him guide you. Move slowly, and if he shows any signs that he's uneasy, back off."

Painfully slow, she stretched out her hand. The large horse's sunken hollows above his dull eyes snuffled it gently. Encouraged, she took a tiny step forward and then, when there was no reaction, another. Amusement filled Wyatt at the sight of the woman, made to look small by the size of the horse's head that was nearly half her height.

"Oh, darling. What did they do to you?" The anguished sympathy in her voice made his heart clench. Now closer, she'd have seen the extent of his mistreatment. Maximus was nothing but skin and bones with deep welts along his side. And where the proud feathers of his breed should have covered his lower legs, there was nothing but scabs.

"I'm hopeful that when the vet arrives, he'll say that it's nothing that time and good treatment won't fix. Otherwise..." He left the unspoken words hanging between them.

Her eyes clouded in understanding. "What you're doing here? It's pretty special."

The sound of a car pulling up diverted his attention, breaking the spell between them. "I think that's the vet now."

"I guess that's my cue to leave." Slowly, Kelly reached a hand out to ever so gently stroke the rough-haired face of the horse. Surely Wyatt imagined Maximus closing his eyes at her touch. "Thank you for letting me get to know you, Maximus. And I promise, if you're good to Wyatt, next time I'll bring you a nice apple." She snuck a sideways glance at Wyatt. "At least, if I'm allowed to."

"I'm sure we can come to some sort of arrangement." He hoped his smile was casual, not showing a hint of the confusion that rocked him at his reaction to her request.

The vet entered the barn, carrying his toolbox of supplies with him. "You're lucky I came out with what you owe me," he said by way of greeting.

"I told you I would pay it off," Wyatt said defensively, the knot that had loosened while he'd shown Kelly around tightening up again.

"I know you're doing good work here and that's why I come. But I need you to start putting more money on your bill than you add to it each month."

"Wyatt, is there something I can help with?" Kelly interrupted. *Why did she have to be here?*

"No. I know where your priorities lie with spending money and it sure as heck isn't on something worthwhile." Hurt flared in her eyes, heat flooding her face as anger chased it away. *What a total jerk thing to say.* A sour taste filled Wyatt's mouth, regret hitting him almost instantly.

Her mouth flattened into a thin line. "Thank you for showing me around. I'm sure I can show myself out."

"Kelly," he called, knowing he needed to make things right. This side that he'd seen of her, it had been there the whole time, and now that he'd had a glimpse, he wasn't sure if once was enough. Her ramrod-straight back disappeared out of the barn. Sighing, Wyatt raked his fingers through his hair. "The patient is this way."

CHAPTER 9

There was no escaping it, he owed Kelly one heck of an apology. There were no two ways around it, and he needed to do it before she headed back to Vegas. Wyatt sat in his truck, trying to psych himself up for the chewing out he would no doubt receive as soon as he set foot into Jackson's house, and the gorgeous blonde who was staying there.

He didn't like to remember the way she'd looked at him. The tough as nails woman in that moment had resembled a kicked puppy. And he'd felt just as bad. Muttering a few choice words, he reached across to the passenger side and picked up the bunch of white tulips he'd collected from town. There'd been something about their stately pale beauty that had reminded him of Kelly. Pushing his door open a little harder than was absolutely necessary, he marched across the frosty yard, the light snow of yesterday having already melted.

Wyatt's knees almost buckled in relief when Jackson answered the door. "You're a brave man coming here," he greeted him. "Those two girls have been locked up in the bedroom for the better part of the day, only coming out for cups of hot cocoa. When I pressed my ear against the door, I heard your name mentioned quite a few times and none of them were flattering."

"What were you doing pressing your ear against the door?" Wyatt gave him a sidelong glance of utter disbelief.

Jackson looked shamefaced. "I was just checking that they were all right." He closed the door behind him and headed to the kitchen. "What did you do this time? It must be bad if you're bringing flowers around to my house. I thought you said flowers were a waste of money. Or is what you did that bad?"

Wyatt accepted the cup of coffee his friend handed to him. He didn't even know how to explain the previous day. It was so at odds with how he and Kelly had been interacting with each other up to that point. "Well." He carefully put the tulips on the bench. "Somehow, and I'm still not sure exactly how or why, but I saw this other side of Kelly and then decided to be a jerk to her."

"I never did understand your way with women." Jackson shook his head. "Guess I better let them know you're here." As he walked past, he laid a sympathetic hand on Wyatt's shoulder, leaving him feeling like a dead man walking. Wyatt took a bracing slurp of coffee, hoping the caffeine would help settle the nerves bouncing around his belly.

Angry stamping feet heralded the arrival of a clearly furious Quinn. "Do you have any idea how long it took me to get her to try to be nice to you? And the minute she does, you become an even bigger jerk than before." Wyatt leaned back away from the aggressively wagging finger in his face.

Honestly, he knew he'd messed up. But it had been a single harsh comment. *Haven't I said worse to her before?*

"Look, I'm sorry, and that's why I'm here to apologize." He picked up the tulips. "See? I even bought flowers."

Quinn sniffed, slightly mollified. "Well, she's up in the guest bedroom if you want to see her." Her face softened ever so slightly. "Look, I know Kelly seems like this hard-nosed doesn't-care chick, but that's all just an act. It's her armor, and I don't know what made her let her guard down yesterday, but she did, and it really hurt her."

Wyatt hadn't thought it possible to feel worse, but Quinn had shown him it was. "I understand. I'm going up to see her now." He made his way up the stairs, each step getting slower than the last as the door at the end of the hall approached, much too rapidly for his liking. He gave a gentle rap, his knuckles barely touching the timber, before pushing the door open.

Inside Kelly sat on the bed, Duchess stretched supine across her lap. The feline fixed him with a hostile glare at his approach. He held the flowers out awkwardly. "I got these for you."

"You don't think that was a waste of money? After all, you have much more important things to spend it on than the rest of us mere mortals." Wyatt winced at the caustic tone. *I'm going to have to eat a lot of humble pie.*

"I deserve that. And Kelly—" He risked taking a seat on the bed. The look leveled at him from both cat and woman had him shooting back to his feet. "I'm sorry, Kelly. You didn't deserve that comment and it was unfair of me to say it."

"You were a jerk."

"Yes, I was."

"I was even nice to you."

"Yes, you were."

"And I'm not usually nice to you."

"No, you're not."

"Fine. I'm tired of wallowing in self-pity anyway. But I want you to know the biggest reason is I don't want to ruin Quinn and Jackson's wedding with our bad behavior. It's really starting to stress Quinn out." Kelly stroked Duchess's head.

"Do you have plans for tomorrow?" Wyatt asked, feeling slightly jealous as the cat closed its eyes in bliss, her loud, rumbling purr filling the room.

"Well, I do need to start booking my Bora Bora holiday."

"Oh, when are you planning on going?" Wyatt transferred his gaze from the cat to Kelly's face.

"I go there every year for Christmas. With the wedding being when it is, it means I need to leave straight after the reception." She spoke eagerly as though the idea of escaping so quickly after the wedding was something to look forward to.

"Don't you think you're being selfish?" His tone was coolly disapproving.

"I don't see how. It's how I always spend my Christmas." Kelly lifted her chin, meeting his icy glare head on.

"It's no way to spend it." Wyatt could hear how sullen he sounded, but an anger boiled and frothed in him. He was dimly aware that it was being directed at the wrong person, but he was powerless against the current of the emotion.

Kelly glared haughtily down her nose at him. "Have you ever tried? If not, then you're in no position to judge."

"You're just being a spoiled princess. You're going to wreck their wedding."

"How?" Her mouth twisted in derision. "Quinn and Jackson will be leaving for their honeymoon. I'll have finished helping organize everything. It's not like you're going to miss me." She blinked. "Or are you?"

Wyatt's eyes dropped to the floor. *What is wrong with me?* "I owe you another apology."

"It's becoming a bit of a habit, and one I don't particularly enjoy," she said softly. "It's tiring. I battle enough with men for my job, I don't need it from you, too."

It wasn't her fault, but how could he tell her the truth? That he lies awake at night, no longer able to sleep under the burden of the debt he's in, the fear of losing everything and then worrying about where the horses in his care would go? Or worse, the ones that were still out there needing him? The strain of trying to act like everything was all right because he didn't want to ruin this special time for his best friend, and having to come up with money he didn't have to cover best man events like the one in Vegas only to see people throw money around like it didn't matter? *Lord, I'm so tired. So tired of everything.*

A gentle warm hand touched his leg, comforting in its weight. It had been so long since Wyatt had felt simple human contact that he marveled at the experience. "Are you okay, Wyatt?" *I wonder if she even knows how much that means to me.*

"I'm trying to be. But I also want you to know it's me, not you."

Those full lips quirked to one side. "Oh, the old it's-not-you-it's-me line. Okay."

He blew out his cheeks. "But it's true. I'm sorry, Kelly. I don't know if you have time, but I know Maximus would really like to see you again before you leave."

Kelly's eyes glowed warmly at the mention of the neglected Clydesdale. "I leave tomorrow afternoon, but if it's all right with you, I can pop over in the morning. I'd love to see Maximus again, too. It's funny, I'm not usually much of an animal person."

Wyatt looked down at the blissfully snoozing cat on her

lap before returning his gaze back to her, brow raised. "Really?"

She laughed. "I didn't have a say with this furball. Believe me, I tried and failed miserably."

"I'm going to go now before I can say anything else to ruin our peace. See you tomorrow?"

Kelly smiled—a smile that made Wyatt feel like a million dollars. "See you tomorrow."

Wyatt floated out of the house and into his truck on a warm glow of happiness. Heck, he wasn't even sure if he'd said goodbye to Jackson and Quinn. But it didn't matter. All that mattered was the fact that Kelly had smiled at him and he was going to make sure she always found a reason to keep doing it.

ALL SHE COULD SEE POKING out from the stall was a large, slightly pale pink nose with its rather fetching white mustache. Kelly looked around confused, trying to locate the source of a low warbling sound. She peered back at Maximus to see his nostrils twitching. *It's the big guy saying hello to me.* She quickly blinked away the tears that sprung to her eyes. Maximus had been abused and neglected by humans and still he didn't hold that against her. Animals really were too good for people.

"I think he's been waiting for you." Wyatt stepped out from the tack room, some strapping and a toolbox in his hands.

"He looks a little brighter. What did the vet say?"

Wyatt's face darkened at the mention of the vet. "He has some skin conditions that we need to take care of and a heavy worm burden that he's had his first treatment for. It's going to take a long time to get him back to a good weight because he's just a massive horse. But slow and steady, and we'll get there." He put his equipment down. "In fact, I'm just about to give him an antibacterial wash if you want to help."

"Sure. What do you need me to do?" Kelly stepped closer, saddened when Maximus retreated back into the stall.

"There's a bucket in the room back there. Can you fill it with some warm water? I'll get a halter on him, and then we can start."

Kelly looked down at the apple in her hand. "Do you think I can give this to him first? You know, while we're still friends?" Wyatt's laugh was marvelous and catching. She couldn't help but join him. "I'm serious. He might not like me after I help you."

The laughter seemed to have wiped ten years off Wyatt's face. *He really is an attractively rugged-looking man.* "I know you are. I think you'll still be friends afterwards, but if it makes you feel better, how about you give him the apple and tell him everything's going to be all right, and I'll go get the bucket."

"Okay." Kelly slowly walked the final steps toward the stall door. Inside, Maximus stood, head low in the corner as if hiding. Her throat thickened as she saw the marks all over his emancipated body. *Poor baby.* "Hey, big boy. I'm not going to hurt you, and I promise no one will ever hurt you again." She looked around to see if Wyatt was near her and, satisfied that he was off filling the bucket, lowered her voice. "You are in the best hands a horse could ever hope for. I know he seems a bit rough around the edges, but I know he will never let anything happen to you again."

In her heart, she knew it was true. Wyatt was a good man. Slowly, as if undecided, Maximus rocked his weight from one hind leg to another, his ears twitching in her direction.

"Don't get shy now. You let me pet you last time and we'd

only just met. And you can't tell me you didn't know it was me when you were being all cute and calling to me."

Satisfaction warmed her as the great horse turned and shuffled his way to her. He stopped close enough so he could reach the apple she held out to him, stretching his neck to its limit to gently lip it from her hand. "Now that's my big, brave boy," she crooned.

"How are you going with the patient?" Maximus tucked his head back into the stall at Wyatt's approach.

"Good. He's a very brave, good boy."

"I'm going to go in there and get a halter on him. I think it's best you stay out here while I do that. He's still wary of people, and with a horse that size, if he decides he doesn't want us in his space, it can end up with one or both of us getting hurt."

Kelly looked at Maximus's sad eyes, not being able to imagine him reacting violently to them. But Wyatt was the expert, after all. "Sounds fair."

Calmly, Wyatt opened the stall door and stepped inside, Maximus backed up until his rump hit the far wall. "It's okay, big fella. I know this isn't your favorite thing and honestly I don't really like doing it myself, but we need to do it to make you healthy," Wyatt said as he slowly made his way over to the Clydesdale. Never once did Maximus take his eye off the approaching cowboy. Kelly found that she was holding her breath as Wyatt slipped the halter into place and secured it. With a little cluck and pressure on the lead rope, Maximus followed Wyatt over to her.

"Such a brave boy," she said. Gosh, but she was proud of that horse.

"What I want you to do is hold the lead rope for me while I sponge some of this wash on him. Just keep talking to him."

"Well, I think that we are going to have one handsome boy on our hands here in no time," she crooned.

"Thanks, I made a special effort today."

Kelly quickly stifled her giggle, afraid she would scare Maximus with her mirth. "I was talking to the horse, and I'm pretty sure you look exactly the same as when I saw you yesterday."

"I did happen to get a discount on these shirts, and I think they really make my eyes pop," Wyatt said modestly.

"If you say so, cowboy." Laughter rippled through her voice. "Let's see, what else, Maximus? Um, it's going to be Christmas soon. Do horses have Christmas?"

"They do on this ranch."

Wyatt's words shocked her. *I wonder who he spends his with?* "So, what is Christmas on the Hope Springs Horse Rescue Ranch like?"

He continued to gently sponge the liquid over the horse's welts. "Well, I go and find a tree and decorate it here in the barn as well as a smaller one for the house."

Kelly arched a brow. "Really?"

"Yes, really. And I'll have you know, I cook a great turkey with all the trimmings." He returned her look steadily, daring her not to believe him.

"Wow, I did not expect that. Does all your family come over?"

His expression, having thawed slightly, became shuttered. "No, it's just me and the horses. Later in the day, I sometimes go over to the Gregory's."

Kelly fought the urge to give him a hug. There was so much pain in his words and something more than he was saying. "You must really love Christmas."

"I really do. Ever since I was little, I've loved Christmas. It's like a chance to start over new, to believe in happiness and joy, you know?" The way he looked at her, she wanted to believe, too. It was a shame she didn't.

"Yeah, Christmas hasn't really been my thing since I was, like, five years old."

"Yeah, your thing's more Bora Bora."

"Exactly." She didn't add that she spent it like him—quite often alone. The only difference was that he had his horses.

Wyatt gave Maximus one final swab and put the sponge back into the bucket. "I think we're all done here. I'd like to thank my able assistant, Miss Hutchinson, for all of her help today."

Kelly gave a little bob, causing the horse's eyes to widen slightly, but thankfully no other reaction. "You're more than welcome."

Wyatt handed the bucket over the stall door to her and removed the halter before stepping out. "I think a couple more days and we can stop doing this and just use the ointment the vet left us."

"Wyatt, the other day with the vet, he mentioned a bill that you owed." It had niggled at Kelly ever since the incident. She firmly believed that what Wyatt was doing here was worthwhile and maybe there was some way she could help.

"I've taken care of it," he brusquely replied, picking up the bucket and stalking back to the tack room to empty it.

Kelly hurried after him and laid a steadying hand on his arm. "I'm glad to hear that, but if there is anything I can ever do to help—this place, what you do, it's amazing." There was a pensive shimmer in the shadow of his striking blue eyes, as if he wanted desperately to say something. Kelly found herself holding her breath. *Please, Wyatt. Let me in.*

A thin smile appeared that didn't quite reach his eyes. "I'm doing okay, but if I ever need help, I'll be sure to let you know." He looked down at her hand where it still rested on his arm.

Kelly followed his gaze, her gut telling her that he was

holding something back, but in that moment feeling oddly connected to him. Wyatt's eyes caught and held hers, feeling like he was probing into her very soul. A frisson of energy flowed up from where they touched, and Kelly found herself rocked to the core. The way his eyes darkened, she was certain he felt something, too.

CHAPTER 10

The slippery potato skidded out of Kelly's hand across the table, escaping the peeler she held. Quinn picked it up and handed it back to her. All of the Gregory women were in the kitchen of Grandma's house preparing the last of the Thanksgiving meal. Some of the dishes were completely foreign to Kelly, and she was intensely curious to know what they were going to taste like.

"I can't believe how rude Markus was when we left," Quinn continued on with her conversation.

Kelly shrugged. It was Markus, after all. It's not like he a cared a bit for the niceties that most people observed as the social norm. "What did you expect?"

"That you put long hours in and that you are allowed time away from The Chimera. That man makes me so mad." Quinn huffed, indignant on her friend's behalf.

"Well, he's going to have to deal with me having more time off. I still have your wedding."

"I think your boss sounds like a jerk," Laura piped up from the other side of the table.

"Laura, hush," her mother said. "Do you think we have enough potatoes now?" Beth asked Grandma.

"I think we should be fine. If you ladies want to start washing up, it will save us some mess after the meal. It always seems like no one wants to help with the dishes then." The old lady's eyes sparkled. Clearly this was a longstanding event that she didn't mind as much as she made out.

"Laura and I can do it," volunteered Beth.

"Mom," groaned Laura.

Her mother ignored her. "The rest of you can join the menfolk. Get them to turn on the Macy Thanksgiving Parade. There should still be some left to watch."

Kelly trailed Quinn out into the living room. The only space left for them was between Jackson and Wyatt. Her friend quickly took the one closest to her fiancé, leaving Kelly to sit beside Wyatt. The parade was already on the television, which surprised her. She couldn't imagine her stepdad watching it. Kelly found Wyatt's proximity both exciting and disquieting. Through the fabric of her pants she could feel the heat of Wyatt's body. *Have I ever been this close to him before?* She gave a mental shake of her head. *More like pistols at dawn, except for that last time we touched...*

"You finally escaped Grandma," Wyatt said, a ripple of amusement through his voice.

"I actually didn't mind," she said lightly. "I've never had a proper Thanksgiving before."

His brow furrowed, and he stared at her baffled. "I thought you and Quinn were both in Vegas last year."

"Yeah, we were. But Marie—you have to meet her—what that woman can do with sugar is lifechanging. Do you remember Quinn's birthday cake? The one I brought all the way from Vegas with me when we first met?"

"How could I forget?" he replied dryly. "I still wake up at night in a cold sweat thinking about the day I met you."

"Very funny." She tapped him lightly on the thigh in mocking rebuke. An intensity darkened his eyes, causing a slight shiver to dance up her spine. *Best to ignore that particular reaction. Now, where was I?* "Well, that was her work. Anyway, Marie made sure we got some slices of these fancy pecan pies and we just had Thanksgiving in our suite and the kitchen sent up a lunch for us with some turkey and sides."

"I still dream about that pie," Quinn added from her other side, oblivious to any interplay between Kelly and Wyatt. "Seriously, I don't know how she takes things like that and makes them next level, but she does, every single time. I'm so glad she agreed to make my wedding cake."

"Our wedding cake," Jackson corrected. "You're going to let me have a slice, aren't you?"

"Hmm, I haven't really decided yet," Quinn teased.

"And you're lucky that you have a mule in me to bring it out for you," Kelly said. The warmth that had started where she was touching Wyatt was creeping to the rest of body. *Seriously, girl, you need to get a grip.* Kelly tried to focus on the parade, but her attention kept drifting back to the cowboy beside her. It was a sweet relief when Grandma finally announced that everything was set for Thanksgiving Dinner.

Grandma had explained the Gregory tradition that only her and the children were allowed to decorate the dining room, and everyone else got to see it for the first time as they filed in for the meal. Kelly had to give the old lady extra points for going for maximum dramatic effect. As she followed Wyatt in, she got her first glimpse. *It looks exactly like the movies I used to watch of American families having Thanksgiving!*

A beautiful tablecloth covered the table. As Kelly stepped closer, she saw that it looked to be hand embroidered with scenes of Pilgrims and Indians. "I made it for the first

Thanksgiving Grandpa and I ever had together," Grandma said, following Kelly's riveted gaze.

Kelly was overawed by the sense of tradition and family that filled the room as four generations of Gregory's and a few adopted ones took their place at the table. "I did the cornucopia this year," Jimmy announced, puffing his chest out proudly.

Confusion must have shown on Kelly's face because Wyatt leaned closer. "It's that thing in the center of the table that has all that stuff spilling out of it," he whispered, his breath warm against the delicate skin of her ear.

Kelly found herself momentarily at a loss to even think of what they had been talking about, his closeness sending delicious warmth flooding through her. Blinking, she focused on the table setting again and saw the object in question surrounded by mini pumpkins, squash, dried corn and gourds. She quickly took her place at the table, surprised at the disappointment she felt when Wyatt chose to take the seat opposite her rather than next to her.

Grandma cleared her throat, ensuring all eyes were on her again, and all thoughts Kelly had of Wyatt fled in the face of the most mouth-watering procession. One at a time, Grandma, Hannah, Beth, Laura and, to Kelly's surprise, Quinn brought in dishes and solemnly set them on the table. "It's the honor of the Gregory women to bring in the food," Wyatt explained. She looked at her proudly beaming friend standing with the women. She was as good as a Gregory now. It didn't matter that they hadn't had the wedding yet. Kelly blinked away the burning in her eyes.

"Everyone, please eat," Grandma said.

And thus began one of the most memorable feasts Kelly had ever had the privilege of partaking in—and she'd been to some truly spectacular events in her time. Turkey and glazed ham, mashed potatoes and candied yams, gravy and cornbread, green beans and stuffing and cranberry sauce. Conversation flowed easily around the table and Kelly couldn't remember when she'd ever felt so at ease. Just when she'd thought she couldn't possibly fit another thing in, the women began to clear away the dishes. She stood to help and was firmly told to sit and then, the icing on the cake, the pies were brought to the table. Pumpkin, pecan and sweet potato pies.

She discreetly shifted in her seat, trying to redistribute the food she'd consumed around in her belly to make more room. There was no way she was missing out on trying each of the pies.

Finally, spooning the last morsel of cream-topped decadence into her mouth, she gave a contented sigh and pushed her plate away. "I'm done."

Wyatt stared at her and then burst out in laughter. "I was beginning to think you have a black hole for a stomach."

"I didn't want to be rude after all the effort everyone went to." Kelly poked her tongue out at him before her sense of humor took over and she laughed. She let out a long, contented sigh. *Darn, but it felt good to just enjoy the moment.*

"Kelly once won a lamington eating contest back in Australia," Quinn said.

"What's a lamington?" asked Laura.

"A chocolate and coconut covered sponge square," Quinn explained, holding her index finger and thumb several inches about. "About this big."

"How many did you eat?" Jimmy's young eyes were wide. The kid was clearly waiting to be impressed.

"Thirteen in two minutes." Kelly modestly buffed her nails on her shirt.

"Really?" burst out Jackson, fine lines dancing around his eyes as he grinned at her, impressed. "That's a good effort."

"What can I say? I'm full of hidden talents." Kelly rather

enjoyed the intense astonishment on Wyatt's face. *So sure he has me all figured out. Chew on that for a bit.*

"Well it's time for us to go set up the afternoon's competition." Grandpa pushed his chair back and rose.

"Can we do an eating one this year?" Jimmy's eyes glowed, the boy had clearly been inspired from Kelly.

Hannah groaned. "Child, how can you fit anything else in after everything you've eaten?"

"Mom says I'm a growing boy." The adults laughed as they meandered to gather their coats and headed to the barn. Kelly wasn't exactly sure what to expect. It certainly wasn't the target they set up, nor the hatchets they lay on a small stool.

"Should I be worried?" she asked as casually as she could manage.

"The Gregory's always finish their Thanksgiving festivities with a nice friendly competition of hatchet tossing." A faint light twinkled in the depths of Jackson's eyes, and she wasn't entirely sure if he was teasing her or not.

Sure enough, he was telling the truth, and a very spirited, intensely contested, hatchet tossing competition began. Kelly joined in, feeling like she had landed into some strange movie but nonetheless laughing and, rather surprisingly, even managing to hit the target a few times.

After her turn, she looked around to see Wyatt, phone to his ear, leaving the barn. *There's no way he's leaving without saying goodbye to me.* Determinedly, she set off after him.

His frustrated voice floated behind him. "You can't take it. It's not your ranch." A pause. "Yes, I understand that. I've started making payments and I'll have the rest to you in a bit." More silence. "Thank you. I promise I'll get it to you by then."

"I couldn't help but overhear. Are you in trouble?"

He whirled around, his blue eyes like hard pieces of sapphire, mouth set in a thin line.

"You couldn't help but overhear?" Wyatt snarled. "You conveniently forgot to add that you followed me out." Her expression hardened, but unlike the last time he'd snapped at her, she didn't seem upset. She seemed determined. He raked his fingers through his hair. "Sorry, I'm not angry at you." *I'm angry at myself. How could I let it get to this?* Bitter remorse turned his stomach and made him nauseous, the Thanksgiving meal threatening to evacuate his stomach. "I owe a lot of money to the bank. If I don't pay up, they're going to take the ranch away from me." He couldn't look at her, he didn't want to see the pity he knew would be shining from her eyes.

"I don't think so. Not on my bloody watch." Kelly's voice rang with conviction. Wyatt's shocked gaze flew to her and he could do nothing more than stare at the vision before him in mute silence. Her eyes blazed with steely determination. She looked like a fierce avenging angel. "Don't even get me started on not saying anything earlier at any of the numerous times I offered assistance and you threw it back in my face. I never will understand stupid male pride."

"Hey." He was too startled by her no-nonsense, take-no-prisoners attitude to the problem to say anything more. *It's kinda hot.*

"Don't hey me! We don't have time for that rubbish right now. But seriously, you should have told me." Kelly thrust an accusing finger in his face.

For all the world she sounded like a peevish elementary teacher he and Jackson had once had. "Yes, ma'am. But I didn't think you would care."

Her fierce gaze softened at his quietly spoken words. "Of

course I care. I swear you've given me plenty of reasons not to, but I do. Anyway, I wouldn't have asked if I didn't. Now, snap out of it and give me details. I need to know what I'm working with."

"I owe $97,347.92 exactly and the bank said I have till Christmas Eve to get the money to them or they'll take the ranch." He wanted to hang his head that he'd let it get to this, but there was a sense of freedom, a weight lifting off his chest as he admitted the full extent of his troubles. "I can sell my truck, but I don't have anything else of value."

"Don't kid yourself." Wyatt's heart lifted in hope. Maybe he'd forgotten something. Perhaps she'd thought of something else he could sell to raise the funds. "Your truck isn't worth anything. In fact, I reckon you'd have to bloody pay someone to take it."

Wyatt's hopes were immediately dashed. "Harsh."

"True, but"—Kelly rubbed the bridge of her nose —"Christmas Eve is Jackson's and Quinn's wedding."

"You don't think I know that? It's crumby timing." Wyatt couldn't feel any smaller if he tried.

"Do you think you could drive me back to Jackson's? I need to get my tablet. There are plans to make and people to call."

"Do you know someone at the bank?" Wyatt knew she was well connected, but heck, it wasn't a small world. Actually, now that he thought about it, he could see Mr Angus, the bank manager, hanging out in Vegas, trying to act like he was a big man.

Kelly chuckled a dry and cynical sound. "Goodness, no. But Wyatt, this is what I do. I make things happen, and I'm very good at getting people with a lot of cash to part with their money, and most of the time it isn't even for a good cause." Her blue-gray eyes sought his. "And this is for a very good cause. Now, let's go say our goodbyes. I've got work to do."

Obediently, Wyatt trotted after the blonde as she stalked back to the barn. He was impressed with this side of Kelly. For once, she was using her considerable talents for good not evil. *No, that's not fair. She deserves better than how I judge her.* He laughed. *How did I get it so wrong?*

"We don't have time for laughing, Mr Daniels." Kelly didn't even turn her head as she marched forward.

"Sorry, Miss Hutchinson."

"Are you going to tell me what you're laughing about?"

"I thought we didn't have time for that sort of thing."

This time, she swiveled quickly, a familiar look of impatience on her face, hands firmly on her hips. "Wyatt, am I going to have to force it out of you?"

He tried to hide the amusement her reaction sent through him. *Kelly really doesn't like not knowing things.* "I was just thinking how much I really disliked you not so long ago."

Kelly's glance was bemused, a soft curve to those delicate pink lips. "Disliked as in used to? Does that mean you like me now?"

"Something like that." Actually, Wyatt was beginning to think it was more than that, but all the horses on his ranch weren't going to drag that out him.

"Wyatt, all your gushing is liable to turn a girl's head. But we don't have time for this right now." There was a promise in her eyes—speculative, and something Wyatt couldn't quite decipher. But boy, did he want to know more about it when the time was right.

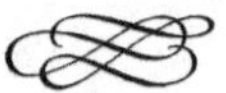

CHAPTER 11

*E*verything happened in a flurry. A quick rushed goodbye to everyone and then Kelly was on the plane back to Las Vegas. A burning sense of purpose blazed from every pore as she sat in front of her computer at her desk, waiting for the other participants to join. Kelly had never noticed before how cold and perfectly ordered her office was. All sleek and hard angles and absolutely everything had a place. She couldn't help but contrast it with the homely weather-beaten warmth that had filled the barn. A beep jerked her gaze to the computer as two squares popped up on the screen, filled with familiar faces and just the people you wanted in your corner when you had a fight on your hands.

"Hello, Misty, Chora, can you guys hear me?" Kelly asked.

"Sure can. Now, do you mind telling us what the big rush for this catch up is all about? I mean it's good to see you and all, but from your messages, it seemed like this wasn't just to shoot the breeze." Misty, all business, steepled her fingers.

"What she means to say is that we're both dying of

curiosity about what you want to talk about with us," Chora added.

"I have a problem and I need your help."

"Fire away. What is it?" Even through the screen, the gleam of interest in Misty's eyes was clearly evident.

Kelly quickly filled them in on Wyatt's ranch, the good he does with the horses and how he was about to lose it all. At the end, she leaned back in her chair, crossing her fingers that they would want to help. She needn't have worried.

"Firstly, of course we will help," Chora assured her. "These horses need the care and home he provides for them. Do you know how he's been managing to pay for everything so far?"

"He pays for it out of his own pocket by working on other people's ranches." Kelly couldn't believe that she'd thought Wyatt was lazy and didn't have a job.

"Okay, he needs to change that, or we will get him out of this pickle and then it will just happen again. He needs to set the ranch up as a registered charity. It will make all future fundraising efforts so much easier for him," Chora pointed out.

Kelly quickly jotted it down. "I should have thought of that myself."

"I wouldn't be so hard on yourself. I've been doing this a long time. I can help guide you through the process he needs to do for that. The next step is figuring out how we can raise the money in the time that we have. Four weeks isn't exactly the longest to arrange something. Misty, do you have any ideas?"

Misty sucked on her bottom lip. "Most people will already have their holiday calendars fully booked up. I don't think hosting a gala would work."

Inspiration struck Kelly. "Maybe we can use the holiday season to our advantage? How about a silent auction set to finish on Christmas Eve to really tap into the spirit of giving?"

Misty nodded approvingly. "I like how you think."

"It could work," Chora agreed. "Wyatt's going to need to provide a spiel about all the good work he does and maybe some stories of the horses."

Kelly tapped her pen. "I can do that for him. And I know one horse in particular that would be a good mascot for the ranch."

"Excellent. It sounds like he's in capable hands. I'm happy to work with him to set up the charity side of things and create a business plan for it going forward. Also, Kelly, a schedule of fundraising events would help, too," Chora said.

"I'll start organizing items for the auction. I'm sure Evelyn will donate some of her sculptures, and I'll also start a list of influential people to invite to it." Misty pursed her lips in thought. "Obviously, Kelly, you'll need to hit up some of the contacts in your little black book as well."

"Already have a list ready to go." Gratitude made Kelly's throat thick. "I don't know how I can thank both of you for this."

"It's what we do. We help animals in need," Misty said. "This is a worthwhile cause, and I'm glad you've allowed us the opportunity to help."

"What she said," Chora added.

"Well, I don't want to take up any more of your time. I'll start on my list and flick through an email with all the details and contacts I have. Chora, I'll also get Wyatt to get in touch with you so he can start on the charity setup. Misty, I'll touch base with you in a few days' time with what I have."

A few quick words of farewell and the screen went blank. A sense of immense satisfaction wrapped itself around Kelly, filling her to her very soul. *Who knew that all the experience I have spent years achieving is almost like it was for this single purpose?* She thought of a blue-eyed, curly black-haired cowboy back in Colorado. *Wyatt is going to be so proud of what I'm doing. I can't wait to hear his voice when he finds out that it's all starting to come together.* She pulled herself up. *I'm not doing this because of what Wyatt thinks. I'm doing this for the animals, especially Maximus.* If her heart mocked the untruth of her thoughts, then she would quite simply not listen to it.

THIS RANCH WAS ALL he had ever known and the one place he'd ever truly felt at home. Every tired timber, worn smooth with age, every rut in the fields, it was a part of him—the very best part of him. A blind panic threatened to pull Wyatt down into its clutches, drowning him until he couldn't draw breath any longer. He hoped that, wherever his grandpa was in heaven, he couldn't see the right mess he'd made of everything.

Slowly, Wyatt led Maximus out to his yard, the horse's ears pricked forward, urging the human holding his lead to step faster. Each heavy hoof that thudded on the hard-packed dirt of the laneway now knew the way, his eagerness telegraphed through each beat he made. More snow had fallen overnight, turning Maximus's yard mushy and slippery in places. But with the clear blue sky overhead, there was no reason to keep the big horse cooped up inside all day.

Wyatt unclipped the lead rope and leaned on the cold steel of the gate as the Clydesdale thundered away, transformed into a fire-breathing dragon. The horse was still way too skinny for his liking, but each day he had more vigor to his step and shine in his eyes. Even his coat where the skin condition had left bald was once again beginning to sprout the finest wisps of hair.

A vibration in the seat of his pants had him fishing his

phone out of his pocket. A quivering coursed through him when he saw it was Kelly.

"Hey, good timing. I'm just out with Maximus letting him have some fun in his yard."

"Really? How's he doing? I miss the big fella so much."

A goofy smile stretched Wyatt's face. His spoiled princess worried about a horse. He shook his head. She wasn't spoiled and never had been. She was just his princess. Wyatt's heart constricted. *His princess.*

"Are you still there?" her concerned voice asked through the phone.

"I've never been better." He gave a laugh, a lightness that could not be contained escaping him. "Would you like to make this a video call so you can see the big guy for yourself?"

"Yes!" Kelly shrieked like a little girl.

He quickly pressed the buttons and found himself gazing at her pale beauty. "You look good."

Kelly's hand flew to her hair, an oddly vulnerable expression on her porcelain features. "Thank you."

Not sure he was ready to take it further, he quickly pulled back to safer territory. "Let me just flip the phone around, you're not going to want to miss this."

With a great grunt and long groaning exhale, Maximus lowered himself on the ground and proceeded to roll, sending great gusts of steam into the air as he flung bits of mud about with his tree trunk thick legs waving toward the sky.

"That's my horse. He picked the muddiest puddle to do that in, too." Kelly giggled.

"Well, you better get yourself on the first plane out here and help me clean him up if you think it's so funny." Wyatt was only partially joking. The thought of seeing Kelly again set his heart to pounding.

"I wish," she breathed, resting her chin in her hand. "I just wanted to let you know that I talked to Chora and Misty and they think they can help."

Some of the tension that had knotted his stomach for so long loosened a little. Maybe he wouldn't have to sell up after all. "That's really great. I appreciate them doing that for me."

"Now, there are no guarantees, but if I know these ladies and the work they do, especially all the charity stuff Misty is involved in, then I think we have a very good chance of keeping the Hope Springs Horse Rescue open. There's going to be a lot of work and it has to be set up properly, but Chora said she would be able to help with all of that."

"I'll do whatever they tell me." He held his hand up in a semblance of a scout's pledge.

Kelly tossed her pale blonde hair back as she laughed. "Why don't you do what I tell you to do? You always insist on arguing every little thing with me."

"I like how pretty you look when your cheeks get all pink and your eyes spit fire at me."

She opened and closed her mouth several times. Wyatt stared at her in absolute amazement. *Have I actually managed to get the last word in?* A pink crept up her cheeks, this time delicate rather than fierce, giving her an otherworldly beauty.

"That's the nicest thing you've ever said to me." There was a softness to her eyes that had so often fixed him with steely resolve.

"Maybe I should make a habit of saying more nice things." Wyatt never wanted to see hurt in those enormous beautiful eyes again, not from words that he so heedlessly tossed at her like knives. "I can't guarantee that I won't still try to get you fired up, but it's time we played nice."

Kelly dropped her gaze. "I'd like that."

"I'd like that, too."

CHAPTER 12

The desk chair squeaked in protest as Wyatt leaned back, harsh in the otherwise silent house. *Heck, I can't remember the last time I spent this much time at this old desk.* As an image focused in his memories, he could see his grandfather, a scotch on the rocks beside him in an ancient glass tumbler as he balanced the accounts for the ranch. *Darn, I miss that old man.* Grief still punched Wyatt hard in his gut, even after all this time. *I wonder what he would make of all this fuss. Probably clip me around the ears and tell me how much of a fool I was to get into this mess, and then he'd help me figure it out. He always had my back no matter what.*

And now Kelly does.

Wyatt could've sworn it was his grandfather's ghost whispering the words in his ear. A shivery trail of goosebumps erupted up his arms. That woman was everywhere. He'd go visit Jackson, and Quinn would tell him about all the things Kelly had arranged for the wedding. He'd met with Chora and started the process of setting up the charity and found that Kelly had already supplied a lot of the information already.

When he'd talked to Misty about some of the items, once again Kelly's name had come up. Somehow, she'd wrangled exclusive behind-the-scenes tickets to meet with the famous country singer, Presley Barnett, and then have her sing a few songs before front row seats at the concert. The one that had surprised him the most was that she'd managed to get her boss to donate A High Roller Experience at The Chimera. From what Jackson had said, the guy was a first-class jerk. It did cross Wyatt's mind that maybe she hadn't asked him and quite simply donated it on the casino's behalf. *Maybe it was best to not pry too much into that one.* Heck, Kelly was even trying to figure out a way for rich folk to virtually adopt a horse and pay for its care and vet bills.

Wyatt had thought that he was going to feel completely out of his depth with Chora and Misty, but they'd been really helpful and genuinely eager to see the ranch—*charity*, he corrected himself—succeed. Absolutely none of it would have been possible without Kelly.

He put his feet on the desk, resting his hands behind his head. *Kelly, beautiful, giving Kelly.* Her strength, energy and passion were at such odds with her cool, delicate façade. Was he kidding himself that, once this was all done, she'd still be as involved in his life? Maybe he could use Maximus as a bribe for her to keep visiting.

The thought of the Clydesdale sobered the euphoria that had washed over him and tangled him up every time he thought about Kelly. An email had come through earlier that another group of horses were in dire straits and, without hesitation, he'd organized to pick them up tomorrow. Now, he just needed to figure out how he was going to pay for the gasoline in his truck for the trip, or if the vet would even accept his call when he got them home. *Kelly, I sure as heck am counting on you to pull this off. We all are.*

Wyatt's gaze lingered on a gold coin in its protective

plastic case against the computer screen. It had been a present to him from his grandfather the first Christmas they'd spent together. Wyatt picked it up, staring at the face cast on the shiny metallic surface. Grandpa had been an avid coin collector and he'd said that this was the one he'd always wanted and had finally managed to get, and he wanted Wyatt to have it. Wyatt had felt like he was a thousand feet tall that day. His hand tightened around it, the hard edge of the plastic cutting into his hand. *Sorry, Grandpa. But if everything goes to plan, it's only for a week or so.*

Pushing away the almost paralyzing fear that he would never see it again, he grimly placed his feet on the floor and grabbed his hat. There was a pawn shop in town that was open twenty-four hours a day. *At least I can get those horses somewhere they'll be safe.* He grabbed hold of that thought like a prayer and forced his way out into the cold, dark night.

IN THE BLINK OF AN EYE, all the Thanksgiving decorations at the casino were packed away and great big fir trees—*real, thank you very much*—festooned with basketball sized baubles were installed around the foyers and many gaming areas. The staff all wore little pieces of red ribbon and faux white fur at the top of their name badges. There was no escaping it. Very soon, it was going to be Christmas, whether Kelly was ready for it or not.

Fueled by steely resolve and a never-ending supply of coffee, Kelly managed to keep all the balls she was responsible for up in the air. She was nonetheless fearful that, with the slightest loss of focus, they would all come crashing down to the ground.

"There's enough space that you can set up a mobile kitchen to one side of the barn." Kelly nodded as she listened to the caterer on the other end of the line. "Yes, early access won't be a problem. Thank you." She hung up the phone, jotting down some notes into her diary. *Quinn owes me so big for dealing with that temperamental prima donna.*

"Excuse me, Kelly? Do you have a minute?" Marie popped her head anxiously in the doorway.

"Of course. What can I do for you?"

"I just wanted to make sure that the design I came up with is what you had in mind. I mean, what Quinn wants, too." The pastry chef grinned at her Freudian slip.

Kelly allowed herself a cheeky answering smile. *Okay, so there might be some truth to that.* She imperiously reached her hand out to see the sketch Marie held in her hand. "Oh my," she breathed, gently tracing the design with a finger. "If I ever get married, you're definitely getting the job of creating the cake."

I mean, I'd have to date someone first. A delicate little flutter took hold of her belly and there Wyatt was again, forcing his way into her thoughts when she least expected it. *Stop being silly. We haven't even been on a date, and I doubt he'd ever ask me anyway.* Kelly caught herself frowning. *Since when have I sat there waiting for something that I want?* She looked up to find Marie giving her a funny look, obviously waiting for an answer to something she'd missed.

"Um, sorry, what?"

"Does this look fit the theme of the wedding?"

Kelly looked at the sketch—three tiers of white buttercream frosting and delicate piping work on the sides to give it the look of snowflakes falling from the sky. In little groups on the top of each tier were clusters made up of fir sprigs, holly leaves and berries and mini pinecones. It had the warmth of Christmas that summed up Jackson and Quinn to a tee. "It's exactly what the theme is all about."

Marie blew her cheeks out, relief melting the tension

from her slight body. "I'm so glad to hear that. The layers of cake will be as follows—first layer, dark chocolate with mascarpone and cherry filling, fruit cake with a brandied cream custard filling for the second, and last, my own special creation, spiced pumpkin cake with cream cheese filling."

Kelly marveled at her creativity. No one even came close to Marie's genius in the kitchen. "Honestly, it sounds like it will taste like Christmas on a plate. The only way you could get it to taste more like it is if you did a turkey, ham and cranberry layer." Marie's eyes narrowed speculatively, and Kelly waved her hands urgently in the air. "I didn't mean that."

"Maybe next time?"

"Yeah." Kelly scrunched her face up. "Maybe next time."

"Awesome. Well, I'll head back and start prepping for dessert in the restaurant. That is, unless you need me for anything else?"

"You've done enough. I can't thank you enough for your work. It's going to be the icing on the cake for Quinn's wedding."

Marie gave an infectious giggle. "I see what you did there."

Kelly's laughter floated up from her throat. "Thank you. I'm kind of impressed with myself, too." She was still chuckling as Marie left the room when a sudden chill chased her mirth away, her good humor fleeing before its onslaught.

"I see you're busy taking up my staff's time with matters that don't relate to this casino, and in time that I'm paying you, as well." Markus's greeting contained a strong note of reproach.

"It was five minutes out of a long day. Chalk it up to a toilet break," Kelly answered with staid calmness. *Where does he get off on criticizing me?* She tensed as heat flushed through her body, riding a wave of anger.

"It's come to my attention that you haven't been as focused on the casino lately as I would like, given what I pay you." His patronizing tone sparked her anger brighter.

She met his accusing eyes without flinching. "That's true. The casino hasn't gotten as much attention from me as it usually has. That's because I was working twenty-hour days, seven days a week, and not complaining once about the lack of personal time." Kelly glared at him with burning reproachful eyes. "And now that I think about it, you weren't exactly heaping praise on me for my selflessness then."

Markus's lips puckered with annoyance. "I pay you a lot of money to do your job."

For a moment, she was breathless with rage at this condescending jerk in front of her. Swallowing down her fury, she smoothed the page of the notebook in front of her. "You have received much, much more than you have paid for since I started working for this casino. You're welcome, by the way. And you know, it didn't bother me before when I didn't have a life outside of The Chimera. Now that's changed. I'm still doing my job to as high a standard as anyone else would do in this role, but if you have an issue with how I'm doing my job, let me know, and I'll pack my bags." She pinned him with an icy look of challenge. "Do you have an issue with me, Markus?"

Grim satisfaction flared when he was the first to drop eye contact. "No, but you only do this other stuff on a break. Understand?" Spinning on the heel of his flawless Italian loafers, he left the room in a gust of expensive aftershave.

Kelly counted to ten to make sure he was well down the hallway before exhaling. Her pent-up breath was fiery with the heat of her anger. *I just won, so shouldn't I be feeling happy instead of this weight of disappointment pressing down on me? I do want this job ... don't I?*

CHAPTER 13

The ginormous LED sign below her on The Strip flashed with Christmas greetings and cheer, truly a behemoth of Christmas spirit punching Kelly right in the face with a not-so-subtle reminder that it was indeed the very brink of being Christmas. Her heart rate accelerated, anxiety mounting that time was slipping away and she still had so much left to do.

Each night as she lay her head down on her pillow after frantically checking and triple checking that she had everything under control, her doubts would paralyze her. Her overwhelming fear that somehow her best wouldn't be enough this time. The one time it really mattered. How could she let this man down? Sighing, she drained her glass of wine and headed to bed for another sleepless night.

KELLY CAREFULLY DEPOSITED the large cake box on the luggage trolley. How the heck she'd managed to get this cake this far in one peace would always be one of life's great mysteries to her. Rubbing her aching arms, she looked around at the only slightly organized chaos that was an airport at Christmastime. Everywhere loved ones rushed into the outstretched arms of waiting family to the cloying sound of generic Christmas carols. *This is why I go to Bora Bora.* Grimly, she gripped the handles of her trolley, thrust it in front of her like a battering ram and made her way toward the arrivals lounge exit.

"What, you didn't see the sign, miss?" a familiar voice rebuked her.

Turning to locate the source, she found Wyatt grinning from ear to ear, holding out a tattered sign with Kelly Hutchinson on it. The thought that he'd somehow managed to keep the original sign made her insides feel all wobbly. "Is that the same sign?"

Wyatt pretended to tug on the brim of his hat. "Yes, ma'am. A good driver never knows when he might need it again, and I knew as soon as I laid eyes on you that you might be one of those annoying repeat customers."

A tinkle of laughter escaped her. "I'm never going to live that down, am I?"

"Not for as long as you live."

There was something in the way he said it, a deeper undertone that made her look askance at him. *I'm just being silly. Of course we will always be in each other's lives. Our best friends are getting married.* She followed him out to his truck, no longer seeing anything but a mode of transportation that enabled Wyatt to do what he needed to for his horses. Somehow it had transformed into a symbol of his commitment, not poverty. Once settled, it wasn't long before the familiar landscape flashed by, now whitened by snow. *Quinn's wedding is going to be perfect.*

"I know you have plenty to do this week, but if you get

time, I know Maximus would really love to see you," Wyatt said.

"I'd love to see him, too." *And spend time with you.* Guiltily, she flicked him a glance from the corner of her eye, afraid her inner thoughts had somehow been projected on her face. "I think Jackson and Quinn might want some alone time before the wedding, too."

"I can make dinner for you if you like," Wyatt blurted in a great gush.

"Before I answer, can you actually cook? And I warn you, opening a can and heating it doesn't count."

Her reaction seemed to amuse him, and he took a hand off the steering wheel and held it to his chest. "It might not be all fancy like you get at your casino, but I think you will find I have adequate skills in the culinary department."

Kelly bit the inside of her lip, trying to picture Wyatt swanning around a kitchen, frilly apron in place and ladle in hand. "Then I accept. Just let me know what day and time. It will also give us a chance to go over any last-minute stuff for the charity auction."

"How about tomorrow? Or is that too soon? We could do it the next night?"

The eagerness in the way he threw options at her made her feel giddy. *Bloody heck, Kelly, you're not some sort of schoolgirl.* "I think maybe the one after tomorrow." She surprised herself with the disappointment she felt at how long she would have to wait to see Wyatt again. "I know that Quinn has a full day of hair and makeup trials tomorrow, and I'm not sure what else after that."

"And I wouldn't want to ruin the surprise of seeing you all done up before the wedding." *If I didn't know better, I would think he sounded like the groom.* Kelly's tummy flip-flopped. *A groom who's eager to see his bride.*

Kelly was still mulling over their conversation long after

she should have been asleep that night. *At least it's taking my mind off stressing about the fundraiser.* She slapped her forehead. *Oh, great work, Kelly. Now I'm thinking about that again.* Groaning, she pulled the cover over her head. *One sheep. Two sheep. Three sheep...*

THE NEXT DAY and night flew by. The day of the makeup and hair trials had been a flurry of champagne and pastries. Honestly, Kelly was thankful that Grandma Gregory had had the forethought to bake them. With the sheer number of bottles the bridal party had gone through, if it hadn't been for the buttery little tarts she'd made, things would have descended into drunken giggles and hijinks long before they did. Quinn's mom and sister-in-law had arrived in time for the day, and her dad and brother had been taken over to spend the day getting to know Jackson and his family better.

As Kelly made her way to bed that night with a fuzzy head, she was vaguely glad that it wasn't too long before she'd be having dinner with Wyatt. In fact, given the way the room spun when she lay down on the bed, forcing her to cling on for dear life, it might be best if she didn't go anywhere for quite some time. Some hours later, when she was forced to madly dash to the bathroom, she decided it had been very wise indeed.

KELLY WAS BEGINNING to reconsider some of her life choices the next day after a round of picking up dresses, running last minute errands, and bouncing on dirt roads. *And they say fresh country living is good for the health. It's not on a hangover!*

At last, just as the light was beginning to fade, she made

her way over to Wyatt's ranch. A light was still on in the barn when she pulled up, casting gleaming puddles onto the snow where it spilled out through the cracks. A wry smile played at her lips. *Of course that's where he would be.* Stepping out of the car, the freshly fallen snow crisp under her boots, she pulled her coat tighter around her body.

"Is anyone here?" she called.

"Perfect timing. I'm just finishing feeding up the horses, if you want to help." Wyatt's head popped out from the feed room when she entered.

She made her way down the aisle, smiling to herself at the hanging Christmas decorations and the large fir tree set against the feed room wall. She found herself on the receiving end of a bucket. "That's Maximus's. Just tip it into his manger but make him wait. He can be a bit pushy around food," Wyatt instructed, hefting three buckets to her one.

"Okay, but if I had been starved, I'd probably have a problem at dinner time, too. Anyway, I can be bossy when I have to be."

Her companion regarded her with amusement. "I know."

Kelly loved this gentle comradery they'd fallen into, the gentle humor and teasing. A sudden rhythmic thudding jerked her eyes forward to catch sight of Maximus's great head nodding as he pawed at the stable door. "All right already, I'm on my way, keep your shoes on."

She set her bucket down and planted her hands firmly on her hips. "You need to back that big head of yours up so I can tip your feed in. Don't make me get all cranky now." Maximus didn't appear to take her seriously, continuing to make a racket. She stepped forward, flapping her hands about in a shooing motion. That seemed to get his attention, since he fixed a baleful eye on her before grudgingly stepping back. "That's much better." Before she could lose the upper hand, she quickly tipped the feed into the manger. "I'd be pretty concerned about getting fed if I'd been starved, too." Kelly reached out and rubbed his neck just under the mane. "But I'll let you in on a little secret. It doesn't matter which day it is, you will always have a full belly here," she whispered.

"Telling secrets?" Wyatt's warmly amused voice from behind her made her jump guiltily.

"That's between Maximus and I," she sassed.

"Oh, I see how it is now. Ganging up on me."

"You love it," Kelly tossed playfully over her shoulder at him.

"I'm really beginning to." Wyatt turned before she could get a clear read of his expression. "Now, Maximus, if I can steal the lady away from you, I believe I have a date with her."

A date? A warmth of confusion flooded her. *Surely he was just using the words figuratively.*

Kelly had never actually stepped foot inside the house with its ever so slightly sagging front porch. It looked sorely in need of a fresh coat of paint and maybe some new roofing. Now it just showed her that there was a barnful of fed and cared for horses, not a sign of Wyatt's negligence. The inside was both exactly and nothing like she'd imagined it would be.

Framed black and white photographs hung on the pale-yellow wallpapered walls, showing an older man and a little boy. There was one of a younger version of the man with a smiling woman and young girl. A crochet rug hung over the back of an old threadbare sofa, the colors long faded. All of that was exactly what Kelly had been expecting. What she hadn't expected were the Christmas ornaments everywhere and the tree that appeared to be straining under the sheer weight of the decorations that festooned it. Eyes incredulously wide, she turned to stare at Wyatt. *Hadn't he said he only had a small tree inside the house?*

"What? So, I like Christmas."

"You really, really do," she agreed. "Is that what you call a little tree?"

"Size is all in the eye of the beholder." Giving her a suspiciously straight-faced look, he turned his back toward her and headed into the kitchen. "I hope you don't mind, I made us a stew."

Curiously, she followed him in. "It sounds yummy."

"I just need to put a salad together. If you want to open a bottle of wine and pour us each a glass, I'll have supper on the table in no time."

Kelly found some glasses and opened the wine, watching Wyatt chop up some vegetables. *Gosh there was something sexy about a man who knew how to cook.* She sipped her wine. *I wonder what else he's good at.*

"So, Christmas is your thing?" Kelly pressed as he set the bowl of salad on the table beside the casserole dish of stew.

"As much as Christmas isn't your thing," he countered as he ladled a mound of steamy meat and gravy onto her plate and then his own. Judging from the narrowed eyes and pursed lips, his reply hadn't dissuaded her line of questioning.

"It's just unexpected." Kelly blew on the morsel of meat skewered on the tines of her fork to cool it. Wyatt found himself distracted by the sight of her puckered lush lips, gently blowing puffs of air out.

"I got it from my grandpa. He loved Christmas."

"Was it your grandpa who raised you?" She delicately placed the food in her mouth, chewing slowly. "This is really good."

"Thank you." Wyatt didn't talk about his childhood at all

if he could help it, but knowing Kelly as he did now, he knew she would be like a dog with a bone till he at least gave her a little information. "My mom, Grandpa's daughter, she was into drugs and all kinds of things. She left the ranch as soon as she could and only came back long enough to leave me here."

The pain of her callous rejection robbed him of breath, his ribs constricting so he felt like he couldn't draw breath. He hated how she still had the power to hurt him, even after a lifetime of absence. Kelly reached out and held his hand. He marveled at how their fingers looked intertwined together, the contrast between her delicate porcelain ones and his big, deeply tanned ones.

"It was probably for the best that Grandpa raised me. Grandma had died a few years earlier, so it was just him and me." Wyatt had spent his whole life worshipping the ground the old man had walked on.

"What was your father like?" Her face was soft with sympathy.

"Dear old Mom never did tell anyone who he was. Heck, she probably didn't know herself." Wyatt cleared his throat. *This is why I never talk about this stuff. It's all best left in the past.* "Anyway, to answer an earlier question, Grandpa loved Christmas because it had been Grandma's favorite holiday of the year, and then I guess with having a kid around, he just kept that going."

"This ranch is the only home you've ever known?" her soothing voice probed further.

"Yeah, and look how good I've done at looking after it." Sour bile of defeat filled his mouth, making the stew inedible. *Why am I telling her all this? She's going to think I'm a crybaby.*

Kelly gripped his hand tightly. "What you've done is protected and cared for animals that couldn't do it for themselves. I'm sure your grandpa is looking down on you proud as punch." There was a fierceness as she spoke, her blue-gray eyes daring him to disagree.

Wyatt cleared his throat again. "I've answered your questions. Now it's time you answer some of mine. Why don't you like Christmas?"

Kelly imperceivably flinched and went to withdraw her hand from his grasp. There was no way that Wyatt was going to let her. Somehow, he knew she needed him to touch her while she spoke as much as he'd needed her to. It had soothed the pain, and he would die before he didn't do the same for her.

"Well, one Christmas Eve, my dad said he was going to pick up some presents. I was five at the time." Her voice was coldly matter of fact, her expression lost in the fog of distant memory. "Well, he must have liked what he found out there a lot better than us because he just never came back. Mom never spoke his name again and, a year later, I had a brand new stepdad who just so happened to be the high-profile barrister Mom had hired to get her divorce from Dad." She reached for her wine glass and gulped down several mouthfuls. "A year after that, the first of my three half-siblings was born." Kelly's glorious eyes shimmered with anguished pain. "Every time I failed at something, my stepdad would tell me it was because I had the blood of my loser father. It didn't help that I was a chubby child either. I worked twice as hard to be accepted, and it turns out, even that wasn't enough."

Wyatt stood abruptly. He couldn't handle seeing this loving generous woman in pain any longer. Gently, he raised her to her feet and gathered her snugly in his arms. His large hands took her face and held it tenderly. "You're the most crazily driven person I've ever met. You're beautiful and smart and being around you makes me feel good inside."

His heart lurched as she raised her shimmering eyes to

meet his, the feelings he felt for her intensifying. Wyatt knew she felt something, too, a rush of pink staining her pale cheeks. Lowering his head, his lips gently brushed against hers, her lips deliciously soft. *After this, there's no going back.* And he didn't care. Pulling her closer to him, he forgot everything but the woman he held in his arms and their kiss.

CHAPTER 14

Several tables had been joined together, spilling from Grandma Gregory's dining room out into the living room to accommodate all of the pre-wedding guests. Kelly's mouth watered at the aromas wafting from the kitchen as she sat, politely making conversation with Lisa and Beth. Somehow she'd managed to end up between the sisters-in-law, but at least it gave her ample opportunity to stare at Wyatt who was sitting across from her yet again. *The man was beginning to make it a habit.* From time to time, she would catch his eye and she'd feel a bond flicker to life between them.

Jackson's dad tapped on his glass with a butter knife and a hush fell over the room. "Jackson's mom keeps getting in my ear and telling me that I need to say something. So, in the interest of continued peace in my marriage, which I'm sure you will appreciate the wisdom of soon enough, Jackson, I've decided it's better for me to be well-trained over defiant." A few chuckles sounded from the married men around the table, quickly stifled when their wives glared at them. "Family is everything to the Gregory's. I think the fact we all

110

decided to live a walking distance from each other vouches for that. Quinn, everyone with eyes can see how much Jackson loves you, and tomorrow you will declare your love for each other before God, and I could not be prouder to call you my daughter-in-law. Welcome to the family." He raised his glass in salute, and the guests followed suit.

"Dad, is that a tear in your eye?" Beth asked, leaning her elbows on the table to get a better look.

"Your mother needs to dust. I must have something in my eye." He dodged the playful punch his wife sent in his direction at his cheekiness.

Kelly was amused to see Mr Williamson reluctantly rise to his feet at his wife's urging. "From the moment the nurse put her in my arms, Quinn's been my baby girl. As a dad, you try to protect your little girl from everything bad in life, and sometimes I wasn't able to do that, to my regret." He choked up, taking a drink to calm his emotions.

"Dad, I don't blame you for anything," Quinn cried.

"I know, but one day you will be a parent and you'll know what it's like. But I don't worry anymore because I know you have Jackson. Your mother and I are so proud of you and love you so much. We feel like we haven't only gained a son-in-law, but a whole another family here in Colorado." Mr Williamson's hand visibly shook as he raised his glass.

Kelly found her gaze straying back to Wyatt, both alone in this world. No family left, or at least none who wanted to claim them. How different their wedding would be. Her eyes flew open wide just as his met hers, a quizzical look making his brow furrow. Kelly shook her head, smiling reassuringly at him, a relieved smile making his eyes sparkle at her from across the table. *Bloody heck, Kelly. Where did that thought come from? One kiss and you're planning the wedding!* She picked up her fork, forcing herself to focus on the conversation around her. *Safer that way.*

~

"I HAVE something I want to give you all," Quinn announced while Jackson was spending the night before the wedding at Wyatt's house. She excitedly ran from the room and returned with gift bags. "I got some for the rest of the bridal party as well." She looked like she was fit to burst.

Kelly pulled out the white tissue paper that had been artistically stuffed in the top of the bag, exposing white silk pajamas with little candy canes all over them. She pulled them out to find a matching kimono. On the back, *Kelly, Maid of Honor* was embroidered in red lettering. "Looks like you're trying to tell me you want a pajama party."

"I have a set for me as well. And I have popcorn, and I think *Mama Mia* is the perfect movie for tonight."

Mrs Williamson pulled her daughter into her arms. "I can't think of anything I'd rather do than have a sleepover for the last night my baby girl is still a Williamson."

Quinn looked at her dad. "Somehow, I didn't think you'd want silky PJ's. Do you like the flannel ones I got you?"

He laughed. "I'm going to be snug as a bug."

"Excellent." Quinn clapped her hands together. "Now, let's get changed, and then I'll get some champagne and popcorn ready."

"Champagne," groaned Kelly, dramatically holding the back of her hand to her forehead. "I'm still recovering from the other day."

"Mimosas then?" Quinn suggested.

"Well, Mimosas are pretty much a health drink, on par with a smoothie, so that should be fine."

"Good, now go get changed." Quinn pointed to the hallway door. Clicking her heels together, Kelly joined the others and obediently trotted off.

When she returned, Quinn was busy pouring drinks, the

others still apparently getting changed. "How's everything with Wyatt?"

Kelly sucked the inside of her cheek, trying to smother the quiver in her belly at the mention of his name. "Good, I think? Did I tell you Evelyn Hart has donated a sculpture and also a one-on-one glass working class with her?"

"I liked Evelyn. I thought she was a really lovely lady."

"She is, and what Misty and Chora have been doing, it's going to help save Wyatt's ranch and all those horses." *I hope.* "But there are still a few last minutes things I need to do tomorrow, which won't in anyway intrude on the wedding," Kelly hastened to add. Her heart beat faster. Usually she thrived, enjoying the electrifying thrill of the pressure. But this time it was different. This time the stakes were unbearably high. The thought of the man she cared about—she didn't dare consider her feelings were more—the thought of Wyatt losing the ranch, the only home he'd ever known and all those horses that needed him, it made her heart twist in a spasm of anguish.

Kelly refocused to find her best friend watching her closely, a hint of a smile ghosting her lips. "Is there anything you want to talk about? You and Wyatt seem to be getting on better these days." Quinn pressed.

"We are," she replied noncommittedly.

"Oh, come on, Kelly." Quinn rolled her eyes dramatically. "I've seen the way he looks at you. It's obvious he's sweet on you."

"We might have kissed." Kelly calmly took a Mimosa off the counter and sipped it as her friend spluttered indignantly.

"How do I look?" Mr Williamson appeared at the kitchen door with perfect timing, holding his arms out and doing a slow spin.

"Fabulous, Mr Williamson," Kelly said.

"Gorgeous, Dad. Can you take this popcorn into the living room?" Quinn handed him two enormous bowls. "I'll be in shortly." Kelly made to follow the food from the room. "Don't you dare. You're not going anywhere till I get answers."

"I thought I'd told you everything." Kelly gazed innocently back at her friend.

"Not by a long shot. When? Where? How?"

"Well, you're the one getting married tomorrow, so I hope you know how kissing works."

"Don't be funny. Details."

"We kissed last night." A delicious warmth enveloped her at the memory.

Quinn sighed dreamily and leaned her weight onto her elbows. "I'm so happy for you guys."

"What do you mean? It was one kiss." A hollow feeling gripped her heart at the trite words, a mute argument to the lie she spoke.

"Kelly Hutchinson"—Quinn straightened, hands firmly on hips—"I've known you for quite a few years and you've never once encouraged romantic gestures from anyone I know of."

"What about my Bora Bora hookups?"

"That's physical. I dare you to tell me that that is all it was with Wyatt and I can tell you it won't have been for him. He's not that type of guy."

It was ridiculous how her heart sang at Quinn's declaration. In that moment, it had felt … right? Like somehow there was someone who understood her and had felt the pain she had. "I like him. But for now, I want to focus on you and tonight. Wow, it's Christmas Eve Eve."

Quinn picked up the tray of drinks. "I can't believe I'm getting married and my maid of honor is already kissing the best man." She giggled at the dark look Kelly leveled at her. "You don't scare me, Kelly, and I'm pretty sure you definitely don't scare Wyatt either." With that final retort, Quinn turned her back on her, leaving Kelly to ride the tsunami of emotions that battered her.

Heck, this is why I avoid men most of the time and feelings in general.

~

"YOU REMEMBER when we were little and your grandpa would let us stay up late to watch those old western movies he used to love so much?" Jackson took a slug of beer, his legs comfortably stretched out in front of him on the coffee table, a fire crackling in the fireplace.

"And your mom would always pack some candy for us because she was just glad that we weren't under her feet for a while." Heck, it felt like a lifetime ago, the carefree bloom of childhood having faded long ago. "I can't believe this is your last night of freedom as a single man. I kinda feel like we should be doing something crazy."

"We are. Look at us wild men." The goofiest grin Wyatt had ever seen stretched his best friend's face comically. "Man, I can't believe it either."

"She's one heck of a girl."

"Quinn is everything. I didn't know that someone like her existed and that she would feel the same way I did about her. I've pretty much used up all my luck for the rest of my life."

Wyatt necked his beer. "You always were a lucky so and so."

Jackson elbowed him none too gently in the ribs. "I'd say you're pretty lucky these days, too."

"I don't know what you mean." Wyatt kept his features neutral. If Jackson got one sniff of weakness, he was never going to hear the end of it.

"That little blonde you used to enjoy fighting with all the

time now seems to be spending a lot of time with you when she's here."

"She's helping with saving the ranch."

Jackson's vexation was clearly evident in the look he leveled at him. "You should have said something before you got in trouble."

Wyatt slouched deeper into the sunken cushions of the sofa, guilt a companion so constant that he would have felt lonely without it always riding at his shoulder. "You and Quinn had just started planning your wedding. I wasn't going to dump all my crappy stuff on you guys."

"But you did with Kelly."

A wry smile. He had him there. "Kelly didn't really give me much of a choice. She was going to help me if I liked it or not." *Darn, but I'm glad she did.*

"She's awfully pretty." Jackson cast a sideways glance at him.

"She's gorgeous."

"And smart."

"And smart."

"So, have you told her you like her yet?"

"I kissed her last night." It was gratifying to watch Jackson spray his beer. *Not so smug now.*

Jackson wiped his mouth on his sleeve. "I guess she knows you like her then."

Did she? They hadn't really talked about feelings after that one moment of shared experience. It had been late, and she'd made her excuses and left. And what would he have said anyway? Did he like her? It didn't seem a strong enough word for the way his soul seemed to recognize her and call out to its kindred spirit.

"Not in so many words."

"A girl like that, I wouldn't hang about too long. I mean, you're already punching above your weight as it is."

Wyatt smoothed down his shirt. "I'll have you know, I'm quite a catch."

"Yeah, well, isn't she off to Bora Bora straight after the reception?"

A stab of fear struck his heart. She'd never mentioned it again. Somehow he'd just figured that, with everything going on with the charity auction for the ranch, she'd decided to skip it this year. A small part of him had fantasized about what spending Christmas snug and cozy here at the ranch, celebrating the survival of this place together, would be like. Heck, in his version, he'd even converted her to be a fan of Christmas. *What if she wasn't going to hang around after all?*

CHAPTER 15

"Have I congratulated you yet on the thoroughly awesome idea it was to hold your wedding just after lunch?" Kelly settled herself into the chair beside Quinn, a hearty plate of food in front of her.

"Jackson suggested it because he reckoned it was going to be the warmest time of the day."

"I'm loving that I went to bed in the wee hours of the morning after a fabulous night of movies and good company and still got a sleep-in before we needed to start getting ready." Kelly peered at her friend. To all outward appearances, she seemed calm. "How are you feeling this morning? Any jitters?"

"No. I feel completely and utterly at peace with life." Quinn's eyes were serene. Kelly fought a stab of envy that her friend had seemingly found the answer to such a deep mystery.

"Well, I'm feeling pretty good about my breakfast." To prove her point, she broke off a piece of waffle and stuck it in her mouth. "Man, I love waffles."

"As much as you love coffee?" Quinn quirked a teasing brow at her, sparkling laughter in her eyes.

"Not gonna make the call, I'm afraid, and you can't make me."

Quinn giggled, her expression sobering as she spied the clock on the wall. "I'd better head for the shower. The hair and makeup lady will be here soon." She fixed an authoritative eye on Kelly. "And if you want a hot shower, I suggest you get in before Dad does."

"As soon as I finish my breakfast, I'll head up. It should give you enough time to finish your shower."

Listening to the various Williamson's moving about the house, the air of anticipation slowly starting to build, Kelly began to check her emails. It was going to be a big day in more ways than one. All she could pray for was that the second part of the day would have as happy an ending as Quinn's wedding.

The house was quick to fill with laughter and love that was almost tangible in the air as everyone began to get ready for this most momentous of days. The photographer arrived and discreetly began to take pictures of the bridal party at the various hair and makeup staging areas that had been set up. Once again, it was impossible for Kelly to not compare the joy of the women present, their happiness to share the special day with Quinn, to what her own wedding day would be like. Irritated, Kelly pushed a stray tendril away from her face. Why was she even thinking about it? The hair stylist, mistaking her frustration, quickly secured it back.

And then, in the blink of an eye, Kelly went upstairs with the ladies of Quinn and Jackson's families to begin the significant task of getting the bride into her dress. "I wonder what Jackson is doing now?" Quinn asked.

"Probably having a pop tart and watching cartoons in his

underwear," Beth laughingly suggested, making a face at her brother's expense.

"Beth, there's no way Jackson is doing that," scolded their mother. "I raised him to have more sense than that. Besides, it's too cold. He'd at least be wearing some clothes."

"I noticed she didn't disagree about the pop tart and cartoons," Kelly whispered to Quinn.

"That's because she knows her son."

I wonder if Wyatt is doing the same. A visual of Wyatt in his underwear was not unappealing. Shaking the thought from her head, she stepped forward. "Okay, ladies, any suggestions on how we get this bride all gussied up?"

THE FIRST THING that hit Wyatt when he followed Jackson into the barn was the smell of Christmas. Fir, cinnamon, nutmeg. His nostrils twitched. He might even detect a hint of cranberry. And then the sheer force of what Kelly had managed to create in a dim, dusty barn hit him. Christmas garlands hung from the end of each row of pews that had been set up in one corner, poinsettias in large ribbon-festooned pots beneath. The aisle was white with borders of red and green that intertwined as they ran the length of it. As he and Jackson made their way up to greet the priest who already stood ready, Wyatt took in the wedding arbor. Boughs of fir spilled down on each side of the raised platform and tall white candles in glass vases were interspersed throughout the greenery. Holly berries and white roses made up the spectacle. From the rafters of the barn, more garlands hung in great ropes, fairy lights glittering.

Wyatt's mouth opened as he looked around, vaguely conscious that Jackson was doing the same. There was a screen made up of closely packed together Christmas trees providing a barrier between where the wedding ceremony was to take place and the reception. Wyatt couldn't even imagine the spectacle that lay behind the trees.

"Holy heck," muttered Jackson in awe.

Wyatt had to agree with him. There was nothing cold or impersonal about the space. There was a magical warmth everywhere that somehow encapsulated the childlike joy of Christmas with the sophistication of adulthood. *Not a single hint of snow queen.*

Slowly and in groups, the guests began to arrive. Wyatt stood with Jackson as the priest conferred some sage last-minute bits of advice for the groom. He adjusted his shirt cuffs and smiled in greeting at Quinn's brother who'd been in charge of calling the girls to make sure they were still on time.

"Mom says they're on their way."

Jackson straightened. "It's finally here."

"How do you feel? Nervous?" Heck, Wyatt was sweating enough bullets for both of them. For some reason, his feet seemed to find it impossible to remain in one place for very long.

"This moment is…" Jackson's gaze turned introspective. "I never knew this moment would feel like this, standing here, waiting for Quinn. I have this profound sense of peace, like this is how it's meant to be." A teasing light filled his eyes as he took in his fidgeting best man. "Are you sure you're not the one getting married today?"

Wyatt resisted the maddening urge to loosen his collar. "I'm just not used to getting all fancied up." The chattering of the guests fell silent and the first strains of melody floated across the air to them. The poignant notes stirred emotions he didn't want to address deep in his heart. Through the opening of the great wooden barn doors, light spilled in. Outside looked like a glowing portal straight from heaven.

From that golden glow, a small slight figure in a scarlet dress stepped through. Jackson's niece, Laura, walked proudly toward them with all the dignity a tween could muster. Wyatt could see Grandpa and Grandma Gregory beaming, albeit a bit watery, as their great-granddaughter took her place at the altar. Next to follow was Lisa and then Beth.

There was a shift in the music, now swelling into a crescendo. The guests leaned forward, straining to capture the first glance of the bride. And then, stepping through the halo of light, Quinn appeared, ethereal in white, her veil a bright nimbus around her. Beside him, Wyatt could hear Jackson's sharp intake of breath. Standing for a moment to allow everyone to fully admire the spectacle, she stepped inside the barn, the doors closing behind her. It was only then that Wyatt could see the white faux fur capelet about her shoulders and matching muff on her hands. He had little doubt that Kelly had coached her to create the unforgettable moment.

From behind her, Kelly stepped forward, unfastening and sliding the capelet from the bride's shoulders and replacing the muff with a bouquet that looked to have the same theme of fir, holly, poinsettia and mini pinecones the bridesmaids had carried. With a whispered word and quick squeeze on Quinn's hand where she held onto her father, Kelly turned and began her own march down the aisle.

It felt like all the air was squeezed from Wyatt's lungs as he stared at the vision gliding down the aisle toward him. The long fitted carmine dress exposed her shoulders, the contrast between the depth of the red and the paleness of flesh striking. Her long pale blonde hair had been arranged in artfully pinned curls, a few tendrils left free to caress her long, elegant neck.

Wyatt swallowed hard, his palms sweating. *I'm so gone I might never recover from this.* And then her glorious eyes under sweeping black lashes caught his, piercing the distance between them, a wealth of emotion in a single glance. He was lost. Later, he would only dimly be able to describe Quinn walking down the aisle on the arm of her proud father, the way Jackson teared up when he was handed his bride, even the words they exchanged that finally made them husband and wife. But he would always be able to describe when Kelly's glittering blue-gray eyes met his. There had been no one else but the two of them.

CHAPTER 16

Contentment, pure and intense, radiated from Kelly's soul. Surveying the guests amicably chatting at their gorgeously decorated tables, she knew she'd delivered the wedding that Quinn had wanted and, more importantly, deserved. From the little fir seedlings in their burlap-covered pots that doubled as both place cards and party favors, to the table centerpieces that were gorgeous Christmas confectioneries of fairy light filled glass baubles hanging from evergreen boughs and poinsettia flowers.

"You look like the cat that's gotten into the cream," Beth said beside her.

"I was just giving myself a pat on the back." Kelly gave a sweeping gesture like a medieval lord surveying her domain. "Every time I do an event, I like to take a moment and make sure I hit the brief one hundred percent."

"Girl, I think you hit it one thousand percent. Remind me to get you to organize my next party."

"I'd love to. Maybe I'll move to Colorado and open my own event management business. I can see it now—no wedding too small, no bar mitzvah too big." Kelly framed an imaginary sign with her hands in the air.

"I love it." Beth giggled. "And I'm sure I know a certain cowboy who would love it if you moved here permanently, too.

Kelly's gaze skittered to where Wyatt sat on the other side of Jackson, deep in conversation with Quinn's brother. There had been a moment when she walked down the aisle, but now she wasn't sure if she'd been imagining it all. *I'm probably making something out of nothing. Seriously, I must have just gotten too caught up in the moment. It is a wedding, after all.*

Her head jerked to the front when a clear ring of someone tapping on a wine glass chimed. At the table in front of them, Mr Williamson stood, waiting for everyone's attention. The proud father had obviously consumed enough Dutch courage to get over his fear of public speaking. "I'm going to keep this short and simple. Quinn, my darling baby girl, you look so beautiful. Your mother and I couldn't be prouder of you." A tremor of emotion shook his words. Kelly dabbed at her own eyes. "Jackson, I don't think Quinn could have found a finer man to fall in love with. Here's to Mr and Mrs Gregory." He toasted, his wineglass held high.

"Looks like I'm next," muttered Wyatt, pushing his chair back. "I've known Jackson all my life and no matter what, he's always had my back. Quinn, you're a lucky woman, because I know he'll have yours just as much—probably more." A little titter of laughter went through the guests. "Just before he went to Vegas last year, we had a big talk. He told me he was tired of the bull rider life on the circuit, that it was lonely and left him feeling unfulfilled. That he was going to retire after the end of the season and concentrate on what really mattered to him. This ranch and his family. And then I get a phone call about this Aussie girl. The one, I might add, who I had had to put up with hearing so much about the previous Christmas." More laughter. "And I remember hanging up that phone knowing that I was going to be sharing my best friend very soon. Quinn, somehow I got lucky, because the woman my best friend fell in love with has become my friend, too." Quinn mouthed a 'Thank you, I love you, too' at him. "If you will raise your glasses, I would like to toast to Mr and Mrs Gregory."

After silence fell again, Wyatt resumed. "Now, I've researched what a best man's speech is meant to cover and the internet has told me that I'm also meant to mention something about the bridesmaids and how pretty they look. In this case, I think you will all agree with me that they look stunning," His eyes sought out Kelly's like the words he spoke were for her alone. "When they walked into the barn, I don't think I have ever seen such a glorious sight." He raised his glass again. "To the bridesmaids."

"To the bridesmaids," roared the assembled guests back. Satisfied, Wyatt sat down again.

All expectant eyes fell now to Kelly. "I take it that's my cue." Drawing in a steadying breath, she rose gracefully to her feet. "I managed to be there both times Quinn and Jackson found each other, and there was an ocean between those meetings, so I like to think I did a job well done."

Quinn giggled beside her. "It's true. She worked hard for that second meeting."

"When I called in a favor that day at the photoshoot, all I wanted to do was get it over and done with. Little did I know that it was going to change two lives. And you guys were lucky. Lightning struck twice, and you were able to find each other. Quinn, you're my best friend." Kelly paused, her voice choking up. "I love you and I'm so happy you found a man who deserves your love and loves you just as much back. To Mr and Mrs Gregory." She raised her glass.

"Oh, Kelly." Quinn pulled her down into a hug as Kelly sniffled. "That was a beautiful speech."

"Well, don't expect me to give one again. I've turned into a big crybaby."

"I promise this is the only wedding of mine you'll ever have to give one at."

As Kelly dabbed at her eyes, careful to not smudge her makeup, she could feel unfathomable cobalt blue eyes contemplating her.

APPLAUSE BROKE out as the newlywed couple came together, their arms lovingly around each other, and gracefully swayed with the music. Well, Quinn was graceful. Jackson just kind of marched on the spot. Kelly smiled and waved at Luciano and Frankie who she'd just spied in the press of guests. She had a soft spot for the big-hearted Brazilian and his blonde Aussie wife.

"I told Jackson he needed to practice before tonight, but he told me he had it under control." There was a trace of laughter in Wyatt's voice at the wooden dancing style of his friend. "The man can't dance, even when he's drunk."

Kelly glanced at his side profile, admiring the strong, chiseled jawline. Tonight, he had his curls tamed. "Are you any better?"

"I'll have you know, I am grace personified." He haughtily waggled his eyebrows at her. "In fact"—he cocked his head at the final notes playing, joining her politely in clapping at the completion of Quinn and Jackson's first dance as a married couple—"I think you're going to have to experience it." He held a hand out to her. "Would the lady care to dance?"

Kelly found herself slipping her hand into his large, work-calloused one. There was something reassuring about the gentle pressure he exerted when he tenderly clasped it. A sense that he knew his own strength but was respectful of her. He pulled her into his arms as they came together, swaying to the music. *He wasn't kidding. He actually has good rhythm.* As they slowly moved as one on the dance floor, she glanced around at the other couples who filled the space. Each time her gaze returned to Wyatt's, she felt her heart turn over in response.

"I just wanted to thank you for everything you're doing for the ranch … and me." Wyatt's voice broke with huskiness. "Do you really think it's going to work?"

"I think that we've done everything we can and, in a few short hours, we're going to know. But I really believe it's going to work." *It just has to.* "Misty and Chora have been keeping tabs on it for me tonight. They said it was their gift to Quinn that I was actually mentally present for her wedding." Kelly gave a wry smile. "As soon as they leave for their honeymoon, I'm headed straight to my computer and taking over." She stopped to find him peering at her intently, a heartrending tenderness in his gaze. Kelly's heart began to hammer in her chest. *He's going to kiss me.*

Wyatt's arms still encircled her, one hand resting on the small of her back, the warmth of his strong arms so male, so bracing. And then he slowly began to lower his head to hers. Kelly felt her eyelids flutter shut in anticipation—

"They're about to cut the cake." Kelly couldn't be sure, but she thought she hurt a hint of amused knowing in Hannah's voice as her eyes snapped open.

Stepping out of the cocoon of Wyatt's embrace, she smiled, the disappointment she felt reflected back at her on his face. He reached out and twined their fingers together, obviously not content to let her go. "I guess it's time we go get some cake."

"I guess so."

"I had something else sweet in mind." The way his gaze lingered on her lips, she had no doubt he was talking about their almost kiss. A tingling heat flared in her belly. For once, words failed her as her cheeks warmed. Watching her flustered response, Wyatt threw back his head and gave a purely masculine laugh. "I guess cake it is, then."

THIS CAKE HAD BETTER BE the best thing I've ever tasted. Wyatt's jaw was set at a mutinous angle as he led Kelly toward the gathered guests. *Because I darn near was about to taste something sweet.* He thought of Kelly's pale, lush lips, and frustration made him rake his free hand through his hair. The triple-decker confection stood pride of place on a table, Jackson and Quinn standing to one side and Grandma Gregory waving everyone to get in close. It sure was a doozy with all the white icing and little Christmas decorations. *Kelly could probably tell you the exact placement of each thing on it and the precise shade of white.*

Funny how that attention to detail used to make him think she was cold and calculating rather than extremely driven and wanting the best for her client or whoever was lucky enough to get her attention. *Funny how perceptions change and, with it, reality. Or is it the other way around? All I know is that I sure as heck lucked out when she decided I was worthy of her attention. I was such a jerk to her.*

Light glinted off the blade of the large knife Jackson and Quinn held up together. With both holding the ribbon-covered handle, they slowly made the first cut in the flawless buttercream. A cheer rose from the guests as a second cut rapidly followed and a large slice was slowly extracted. Both newlyweds took a bite, Jackson making an exaggerated show of enjoyment. *No cake could be that good.* The crowd slowly dispersed as it was announced that cake would be getting served to their tables. Wyatt, keen to get Kelly all to himself again, turned to leave. She gave a little tug on his hand. "I want to say something really quickly to Quinn and Jackson." There was a light of anticipation, a secret that was bubbling away. Curious, he followed her lead.

"Quinn, Jackson, just while I have you guys alone, can I have a moment?" Quinn's brows rose to the rafters, her gaze bouncing from Wyatt's and Kelly's intertwined hands back up to Kelly's face and back again. Frankly, Jackson wasn't much better, perhaps even worse, with a smug knowing smirk on his face.

"Sure," Jackson answered for both of them. "But I do have to say, it looks like you have things well in hand."

Quinn giggled. "I was going to say the same thing."

Wyatt heaved a longsuffering sigh. They just got hitched and now they've turned into painfully smug married people. "Oh, I'm dying with laughter."

Kelly obviously decided to take the high ground and ignore the banter. "I know it's traditional to open presents afterwards, but I just want to give you my present now." She held out an envelope. There was something in the way she gripped it in her fingers, a slight defensiveness that made Wyatt feel protective of her. He gave her hand a gentle squeeze.

Quinn took it with a slight smile and opened it to extract a plastic envelope. She lifted the top to expose some tickets and paperwork. Her eyes growing wide, she quickly pulled her best friend into a hug. "Oh, Kelly, are you sure?" Quinn's eyes shimmered with unshed tears at the gift.

"Yes, I am. This year there's somewhere else I need to be."

"What did she give us?" Jackson tried to peer over his wife's shoulder, attempting to see the gift that had prompted such a watery reaction. Wyatt was doing his level best to the do the same.

"Kelly gave us an all-expenses-paid trip to Bora Bora."

Wyatt's gaze snapped to Kelly, hers steadfastly refusing to meet his. He stood there blank, amazed, and shaken to his core. He knew what that time each year in Bora Bora meant to her.

Jackson pulled Kelly into a bear hug. "Thank you. This gift is amazing."

Kelly smiled at the happy couple. "Your flights do leave in four hours, so after the reception, you both need to get a wiggle on. You'll go from the white snow of Christmas Eve to the white sands of a tropical island for Christmas Day. I've also arranged for the butler who usually looks after me to make sure everything is perfect."

"Kelly, I don't know what to say." Quinn sniffled. "But what are you going to do? I know you hate Christmas."

Kelly finally met Wyatt's eyes, and his whole body filled with a sense of waiting, yearning for something that was just out of reach. "Don't worry about me. I'm going to be exactly where I want to be." She looked back to Quinn. "Now, are you going to let me have a piece of this cake that I had to lug all the way from Vegas?"

Quinn giggled and linked her arm with her best friend. "It's so good I might even have another slice with you."

Wyatt watched the two beautiful women weave their way through the tables, stopping to speak to various guests. He knew he wasn't the intended recipient of her gesture, but his heart told him otherwise. The newlyweds hadn't been the only ones to receive a gift just then, he was sure of it. Now he just needed to decide what he was going to do about it.

CHAPTER 17

"Kelly, I don't know how I can ever thank you for making my wedding so magical." Quinn sniffed. "It was everything I imagined it would be and more. Last Christmas Eve was so special that I didn't think anything would be able to top it. But this Christmas Eve, it was everything I dreamed of."

Kelly dabbed at her eyes with a tissue, already soggy from previous ministrations. "I just wanted to make it Christmas like you wanted. But I've left the best for last. Come on." She grabbed Quinn's hand and hustled to the door, opening it a sliver. "I even arranged for it to snow." Outside, snowflakes gently drifted to the ground, making everything look like a scene from a snow globe.

"Oh, it's perfect." Quinn's face grew serious, her hazel eyes staring intently at her friend. "You're going to be okay, aren't you?"

"Of course. You know me. I don't just crumble in a heap." *Well, maybe, not usually. I'm not sure what I'm going to do if the auction doesn't work. There's no plan B.*

132

"But I also know what this time of the year is like for you. We can always delay going to Bora Bora till after Christmas."

Kelly's heart overflowed with love for her friend, her eyes growing misty. "Don't you dare. I really am going to be fine. I have the auction still to finish tonight and then, well, who knows what I'll do tomorrow. But I do know one thing. You, my dear, will be sitting on a beach drinking a cocktail and making kissy faces at your husband."

"You promise to call me if you need to talk or anything."

"I promise. Now, judging by the look on your husband's face, I think he might be starting to have thoughts about your wedding night."

Quinn gave a tinkling giggle, hand covering her mouth as she flashed innocent eyes at her rapidly approaching cowboy. "Hey, Mr Gregory."

Envy dampened by a tinge of sadness flared as Jackson swung his wife up in his arms and planted a hearty kiss on her. Quinn fanned herself as though she had been left breathless when he gently returned her feet to solid ground.

"Hey, Mrs Gregory. I think I've done all the socializing I care to do this evening. I think I'd like to hang out with just my wife for the rest of the night."

Quinn's cheeks burned brightly, a naughty smile on her face as she fluttered her eyelashes at him. "Why, Mr Gregory, whatever could you mean?" The intensity of the color of her cheeks flamed brighter as Jackson bent and whispered into her ear.

"Sickening, isn't it?" Wyatt's breath was warm against Kelly's neck. Startled, she jumped, having not heard his approach.

She gave him a warning slap on the arm, the muscles hard beneath her hand. "Leave them alone. They're just about to go."

"Right, guess I'll gather everyone up and get them in

place." Wyatt turned and began to signal everyone for their attention. The guests quickly scuttled into place and formed two lines, linking their hands to form an archway.

Kelly gave Quinn and then Jackson a hug. "I'm so happy for you guys. Jackson, make sure she remembers to drink lots of water, and Quinn, with his Colorado winter tan, make sure he puts plenty of sunscreen on." She moved to take her place at the head of the human archway, clasping Wyatt's hands, a quiver surging through her veins, sparking from where their skin touched. She tried to ignore the strange aching in her limbs, smiling as the happy newlyweds dashed past and out into the snowy night to the cheers and catcalls of their jovial guests.

Kelly found her gaze drawn to him. There was no denying that her feelings had deepened into something richer than a passing friendship. She was proud of what he had achieved at the Hope Spring Horse Rescue Ranch and everything, God willing, he was yet to do there. He was the truest person she'd ever met. His wealth wasn't measured by his car or the clothes he wore, but what he gave of himself to his friends, to the horses and, if she was lucky and he felt the same way, to her. *I need to tell him, and I need to tell him tonight.*

"ARE YOU READY TO GO?" There was something lurking in the shadows of Kelly's eyes that made Wyatt's heart hammer in his chest.

"Yep. I'm dying to get my hands on some internet so I can see how the auctions going."

"Even though this auction is important—and I mean, my life at the ranch hinges on it—it's still Christmas Eve and I don't want to forget that. Do you want to come back to the ranch and count down with me? I can't think of anyone else

I'd rather spend the last couple of hours of Christmas Eve with."

I want to be with you when I find out my fate. Every time he saw her, the pull was stronger. Was he going to be able to let her go if she didn't want to stay? The thought of losing the ranch was unbearable, but where would home be if that happened? He stared at the delicate blonde, his heart recognizing that home was right there in front of him.

"I'm a novice at what a real Christmas Eve is like. Maybe you might be able to show me?" Wyatt had never seen such raw vulnerability in Kelly's eyes before. An overwhelming need to pull her close surged through him. Before he could act on the impulse, her expression shuttered.

"I'm sure I can show you the ropes." A fiercely protective need filled him, and he wrapped an arm around her shoulders, pulling her slight body in snug against his. "One thing I do know is this is going to be one of the most memorable Christmas Eves I've ever spent."

Kelly held up her crossed fingers, obviously assuming he meant the auction. "I hope it will be for all the right reasons."

A tingle settled in his stomach. *Me, too.*

THE FRESHLY FALLEN snow and the complete silence gave Wyatt's ranch a sense of pristine perfection. Even the barn that Kelly would have once generously described as ramshackle now had the air of a nativity scene. Goosebumps shivered to life on her arms as she thought about the original Christmas miracle, something she hadn't done for a long time. *I pray that somehow there's another one tonight.*

In solemn accord, Wyatt and Kelly entered the house and she settled down on the sofa to log into the software system for the auction on her tablet. When Wyatt didn't take the spot beside her as she'd anticipated, she looked up to find him standing, looking at the framed family photos on the wall. She stared at his strong profile in acute and loving anxiety. *Please make this all work out.*

As if he felt the force of her gaze on him, he turned his compelling blue eyes to her, an inherent strength in them. There was an air of acceptance to the way his mouth twisted into a wry smile. "If this doesn't end the way we want it to tonight, at least we tried." Kelly tried to keep her tone light.

"Well, in a couple of minutes, we'll know." His quiet, steady words tore at her insides, shattering her heart. "Is it nearly midnight?" Wyatt looked around, startled at the passage of time. He rubbed a hand along his jawline, scratching at the five o'clock shadow that now darkened it. "This day, it feels like everything has changed." Wyatt faltered in the silence that engulfed them, and Kelly wondered if she should reveal her feelings for him.

The screen of her tablet exploded into action. The auction had ended. Now it was time for the reckoning. She flipped the screen down on her lap, hiding the results. "Wyatt, do you want to come and sit with me? It's time."

Wyatt reached out unsteady fingers to gently touch the face of the old man in the picture in front of him —his grandfather—his lips moving soundlessly as though either in prayer or to ask for forgiveness. Kelly couldn't be sure. And on silent feet, his shoulders bowed ever so slightly, he made his way over to her. The cushions sunk lower under his weight, and he took her hand in his, holding it like a drowning man grimly clinging to a life preserver. Kelly could feel the pounding of his pulse at his wrist. *He's terrified.*

"Ready?" she whispered, the words hanging in the air between them.

His glittering blue eyes fastened on hers, a slow tightly controlled nod all he could respond with. Kelly closed her eyes and took a deep steadying breath. *If ever there was going to be a Christmas miracle, now's the time for it. I promise, if you do this for Wyatt, I'll never ever pretend Christmas doesn't exist ever again. But please, do this for him. He's a good man, and I love him.*

Opening her eyes, she hesitantly turned her tablet over, scanning the figures and words quickly. Kelly's hand flew to her mouth. Incredulously, she looked at Wyatt.

"Well? Is that a good wide-eyed look or a bad one? I can't really tell."

"Oh, Wyatt, we did it! All of us. Misty, Chora, you and me." She paused as a notification popped on her screen. "Misty says that she's wiring the money to the bank as we speak. There's even enough money left over to help with some extra things that need to be fixed around the ranch." Kelly paused as another message came through. "Chora says that she has been fielding inquiries about how people can get involved and donate or virtually adopt a horse for a year and cover its expenses."

Wyatt looked stupefied. His features began to blur as a great tsunami of raw emotions buffeted her about. Kelly threw herself into his arms, knowing that he was a safe harbor in the maelstrom.

Suddenly, she was cradled in his strong arms, his hands indefinitely tender on her back. "You did it, Kelly. All of this is because of you," he whispered against her ear.

The floodgates opened and she buried her face into his neck, tears streaming down her face, releasing all the doubt and fears she'd bottled up to keep away from him. Kelly drunk in the comfort of his nearness.

When her sobbing had run its course, she looked up at him, unsure how long he had held her close and allowed her to cry. "I'm sorry, I don't usually cry."

"I don't mind. There's nothing to be sorry for. There's a strength to expressing emotions." Something in his eyes, the softness in the way they gazed back at her, made her heart leap. "I would have lost everything if it wasn't for you. I think meeting you was my Christmas miracle." His words unlocked her heart and soul, a joy so pure that left her euphoric.

"I don't know if I'd go that far. But it was nice using my powers for a good cause, not just some money-making corporation."

Wyatt still hadn't released his hold on her. Kelly hoped he never did. "We make a pretty good team. Maybe you need to adopt Maximus. I know there's always room for you here." He looked up toward the ceiling, his eyes guileless. "Well, look at that. I wonder who could have put that there."

Kelly followed his gaze up, the corners of her mouth tugging upwards when she spied the mistletoe they were sitting under. "Someone who was prepared."

"With a lady like you, I have to keep on my toes. Maybe another Christmas miracle might happen?" Her heart lurched madly at the look on his face.

"What, another one?" Kelly could barely hear her own words over the mad pounding in her chest.

"If I'm very lucky." He brushed a tear from her face with his thumb. "I know what it meant to you to choose to stay here with me. I promise that I will never leave you. That is, if you don't want me to. I love you, Kelly."

Her heart fluttered wildly in her breast. "I love you, too. I've wanted to tell you all day, but somehow there was always something to do."

Wyatt laughed, and Kelly could feel it rumbling in his chest. "Weddings tend to do that. No regrets about not going to Bora Bora?"

"None. I guess it might be time that I see why everyone raves about these white Christmases for myself." She looked up at him from beneath lowered eyelashes, still spiky from her weeping. "Do you know any experts?"

He gently brushed a stray tendril of hair from her face. "I might know someone."

"Yeah?"

"Yeah." His breath was warm and moist against her face, and her skin tingled where his thumb gently traced her cheek. Wyatt's lips brushed against hers, then gently covered her mouth.

"Wyatt?" Her lips whispered against his as she spoke.

"Yeah?" he mumbled.

"Merry Christmas."

"Merry Christmas, my love."

Kelly gave in to the kisses of the cowboy she loved. Finally, she was home for Christmas.

THE END

As an Indie Author, reviews help me get my books noticed. If you enjoyed reading Wyatt's and Kelly's story as much as I did writing it, please leave a review. It will make all the difference to me.

If you loved, *The Cowboy Under The Mistletoe* sign up for my newsletter to get exclusive bonus bits.

Now, turn the page as the Mistletoe Collection continues with Markus's story… *Mistletoe and the Billionaire's Cowgirl*

CHRISTMAS, ST MORITZ

Who says money can't buy happiness? Markus watched the attractive brunette strip down to her bikini to join him in the hot tub. *Merry Christmas to me.* A mere couple of yards from where his hands languidly draped outside of the swirling water, thick snow drifts began, the snow-capped alps majestically rearing up above. *It really did make a man feel like he was insignificant.* Markus's mouth twisted into a smug smirk. *Unless you had enough money to buy those mountains.* Appreciatively, he watched as the woman —*what was her name again?*—seductively dipped a toe in the water before sliding the rest of her lithe body in, the steam thick between them. Although he doubted the distance would last very long.

Somewhere in distant Colorado, Quinn was off getting married to that hick cowboy of hers. It was her loss, really. Who would want to live a life in the muck of livestock when she could have slept on silk sheets every night? *Well, maybe not always sleeping.* And her days would have been spent being pampered. Markus rubbed the bridge of his nose, still irked by her rejection. It wasn't like she was ignorant of what he had to offer. He'd taken precious time to show her, and still she'd acted like he was no one. Heck, last Christmas he'd even bought a casino to show her how much he wanted her.

Never again. He smiled, gesturing for the lovely brunette to come closer. *No names, no promises. That was the way to live life.*

Markus's story, *Mistletoe and the Billionaire's Cowgirl*, is available for purchase on Amazon or free on Kindle Unlimited

ACKNOWLEDGMENTS

A debt of gratitude to my editor Rebekah Groves for her patience with me.

Another big thanks to Megan from Designed with Grace for her cover design.

To my amazing beta readers and street team, you guys rock and I couldn't do it without you. Special mention to Lisa and Cair.

And finally to my fabulous alpha reader Trixie Norman, for all the late nights of reading and endless question about your thoughts.

Buy Now

A cowgirl's heart

An Aussie cowgirl in need. Her childhood friend to the rescue. Can friendship turn into a love story?

Buy Now

A cowgirl's passion

One feisty cowgirl. One steadfast Brazilian bull rider. Will she see what is right in front of her?

Buy Now

A cowgirl's pride

An Aussie cowgirl from the wrong side of the tracks. A handsome equine vet. Can they find a way to have their happy ever after?

Buy Now

A cowgirl's love

A young Aussie cowgirl. A widowed rancher. Does age matter when it comes to love?

Buy Now

A cowgirl's movie star

A fiery cowgirl with big dreams. A movie star far from home. When their two worlds collide, will their love be strong enough to hold them together or will they be pulled apart

Buy Now

A cowgirl's billionaire

A cowgirl adrift. A broken billionaire cowboy. Can he free himself from the past to be the man she needs now?

Buy Now

Billionaire Hearts Ranch Series

February 2021 Release

The wounded cowboy billionaire

Colt's story coming soon

Pre Order Now

The cowboy's billionairess

The billionaire's cowgirl

The cowgirl's fake billionaire marriage

A cowboy's riches (Prequel)

ABOUT THE AUTHOR

Edith MacKenzie or Eddie Mac to her friends is an author of sweet and wholesome contemporary cowboy romance. They say in literary circles to write what you know, and Eddie has certainly taken that to heart. Before embarking on a writing career, she trained horses professionally and brings that wealth of knowledge to her writing.

Now a mum to a boy and girl, as well as wife, she delights with her tales of strong cowgirls and their adventures in finding love. When not weaving the love stories of her characters, she enjoys hanging out with her family and animals, as well as reading, fishing and camping.

Just remember—once a cowgirl, always a cowgirl.

facebook.com/EddieMacAuthor
instagram.com/edith_mackenzie_author
amazon.com/Edith-MacKenzie
bookbub.com/profile/edith-mackenzie

www.ingramcontent.com/pod-product-compliance
Lightning Source LLC
Chambersburg PA
CBHW021201110726
47900CB00002B/676